BACHELOR BEAST

INTERSTELLAR BRIDES® PROGRAM: THE BEASTS - 1

GRACE GOODWIN

GET A FREE BOOK!

JOIN MY MAILING LIST TO BE THE FIRST TO KNOW OF NEW RELEASES, FREE BOOKS, SPECIAL PRICES AND OTHER AUTHOR GIVEAWAYS.

http://freescifiromance.com

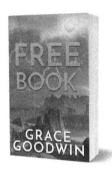

INTERSTELLAR BRIDES® PROGRAM

YOUR mate is out there. Take the test today and discover your perfect match. Are you ready for a sexy alien mate (or two)?

VOLUNTEER NOW!

interstellarbridesprogram.com

1

Warlord Wulf, Interstellar Brides Program Processing Center, Miami, Florida, Earth

"THIS IDEA WAS stupid from the start, and now it's ridiculous," I snarled.

A woman fluttered behind me with a small brush in her hand and brought it up to my neck. It not only tickled, but it was covered in a pale powder she was applying to my skin.

I swatted her away... carefully—she was small and female, and I didn't want to hurt her—then looked back at the comms.

"What is the human doing to your neck?" Maxim asked, cocking his head to the side as if that could help him see better. "Why are your cheeks that color? Are you ill?"

My beast practically snarled, ready to rip the comm screen off the wall. The frustration had been building ever since I'd arrived on this far-off, backward planet.

"It's what they call makeup," I said through gritted teeth. "The small female assures me that if I do not have this red powder on my cheeks, that I will appear to be unwell and weak on the display screens all over this planet."

Rachel, who stood behind Maxim, nodded her head. "That's true. Humans call it stage makeup."

I huffed in disgust and waved the female forward. In moments she was back at it with her little brushes. I looked down at her, tried to calm myself enough not to scare the shit out of her. The look in my eye must have indicated imminent death if she didn't leave me alone. She swallowed hard, then climbed down from the stepladder she had to use to reach my face. I was so much taller than anyone on Earth, and she was a small version of a human. She cleared her throat. "I think that's good enough. Good luck tonight."

"Thank you," I replied, trying to practically whisper so she didn't burst into tears.

She and her ladder scurried away as if she'd used the reserves of her courage to speak to me.

"You look odd," Maxim said. I was glad he refrained from using a more insulting word.

"While makeup is usually a thing Earth women put on their faces, for television, people of both genders need it or they're washed out by the set lights." Rachel explained to Maxim the same thing I'd been told the first day on set.

"I have no idea what any of that means," Maxim said, turning to look up at his mate. He sat in his familiar chair—even though it was light-years away from where I was—and Rachel stood at his side, her arm around his shoulder. It was a very casual pose for an official comms call between planets.

But nothing about why I was on Earth was official or formal. It was a hot mess, as I'd heard someone here say. It was a disaster. The worst solar plasma storm on record had nothing on my life. I was the unlucky fucker chosen for this ridiculous mission because I'd learned the human language of English several years ago. I'd learned it to try to please my Interstellar Bride. My *perfect* matched mate.

Look how that had turned out. Back then I'd been a fierce warlord. Whole. Battle tested. In my fucking prime. Still, she'd taken her thirty days and chosen to return to Earth. She'd chosen another. Not an Atlan, but a human male. A man she'd loved more than she could learn to love me. I'd felt nothing but pain every time I'd been forced to recall this primitive language to speak to the females the Earth program paraded before me like gifts. To speak to the annoying man with large white teeth and stiff hair who took every opportunity to shove a voice amplifier in my face.

I held no hope this mission would save my life. If a perfect matched mate had not ended my mating fever, I had little hope that a stranger would now, even if she were willing. I'd rather return to Atlan and be processed for execution than condemn a female to life with me but without the devotion of my beast.

So far, that dark, primitive side of me, my beast, was simply *not interested*.

"This isn't going to work, Maxim," I repeated. I'd been saying the same thing since the first day I'd arrived. *Three weeks* I'd been on Earth. Three interminable weeks. No wonder females volunteered for the Brides Program to get the hell off this crazy planet.

Their vehicles were primitive and smelled of burned fuel, as did the black tar they spread on their roads. The air was brown with pollution and smelled of chemicals. The people were cruel and unkind to one another, with filthy, unwashed humans left to sicken and die on the sides of streets, sleeping in paper boxes while others lived in palaces of stone and crystal. Earth humans were, as the Coalition had been prior to Prime Nial's decree, unkind to their soldiers who returned from battle damaged. They were ignored or forgotten, denied the honor due them for their service. They were not adored; they were feared. Different.

Like me and every other male and female banished to The Colony. We were damaged goods. Contaminated and shunned out of fear.

Which was one of the reasons I'd agreed to this debacle. Not for me. For them. The others. We needed more brides. Earth females had, for whatever reason, adapted to life on The Colony and accepted our fallen warriors as their own. Claimed them. Loved them. Mated and had children with them. Earth had given us hope, and two of the human mates on The Colony, Lindsey and Rachel, had come up with this insane idea.

Why they believed I would entice human females to apply to be matched specifically to The Colony, I had no idea. I was not the best of us. There were many, many honorable males who would have been happy to be chosen.

But I spoke English, if not very well. I could communicate. Rachel knew I would deny her nothing. She was one of our chosen females, matched to our elected governor, Maxim of Prillon Prime. She was to be honored and protected, in mind and body. When she'd pleaded with me, I could not refuse.

"Can't you try? I know it doesn't work that way, but still. Maybe kiss one of them or something? Maybe that would light the spark."

My beast recoiled at the idea of touching either woman, or kissing them. But Rachel, with her curly brown hair and perky attitude, looked like the hopeful, optimistic Earth female she was. Now, being here and surrounded by females, I understood why she was so small. They were all small. Despite everything I could see wrong with this planet, the humans persisted in their hope. Their optimism. They refused to yield or admit defeat.

"No." One word was all I could give her as I fought back the rage of my beast. He wasn't just uninterested; he was furious at the idea that I might try to force him to kiss a female he did not want for his own. Not now. Not when the fever was riding us like fire in our blood and unrelenting rage was flowing in every fiber of our being every moment of every day. As the humans would say, I was holding on by my fingernails.

"Why not? What do you have to lose? You might be surprised, you know?" Rachel tried to encourage me, and I admired her independent spirit. That spirit was tempered by her two Prillon mates, as theirs were by her. She arched a brow at my statement. "I've heard the ratings are through the roof and everyone's dying to find out what's going to happen next. This is going to be great for recruiting brides."

I set my hands on my hips and took a deep breath, trying not to burst into beast mode. It wasn't because the fever raged within me, but because I was so frustrated and out of control. Here, on Earth, *I had no control*. I ate when they told me to eat. I slept when they told me to sleep. I wore what they told me to wear. I spent time with females they insisted I attempt to woo. I answered to a small, gray-haired human male with a clipboard and dark-rimmed glasses. He was not my commander, not an Atlan. Not a soldier.

He was an executive assistant, whatever the fuck that was supposed to be. As I was not one of these executives, I was uncertain why he insisted on following me from place to place and ordering me around like a small child. Sometimes he even spoke loudly, slowly, as if I were not only contaminated with Hive technology, but deaf and dumb as well.

"I don't care about human ratings," I grumbled.

"But you do care about helping us get more brides to The Colony," Maxim insisted, and he was not wrong so I did not argue. Many worthy males waited for a mate. Too many.

Sadly I knew what the term "ratings" meant and all the other terminology associated with an Earth television program. "Lindsey wanted me to come to Earth to promote alien mates with the hopes of gaining new volunteers to the Brides Program. Fine. That is what I agreed to. They were supposed to interview me. Get some pictures. Send me to the different bride centers around the planet. What you didn't tell me was that I was to be on some kind of... entertainment program experiment."

"Reality TV," Rachel clarified. I could tell by the way she was biting her lip that she was holding in a laugh. She was not my mate, but I wanted to paddle her ass for finding amusement in my discomfort.

I'd learned all about the concept of reality television the moment I stepped off the transport platform when the producer, the director and two staff underlings met me with ridiculous enthusiasm and wide-eyed stares. Turned out, I wasn't a representative from The Colony answering questions about life on the planet and the various fighters who were possible matches. I was a tiny, fat Earth animal with a lot of fur. Once Rachel used the term, I had searched Earth's primitive computer to look up the animal in question. I was, apparently, a rodent kept as a pet by small children. A... guinea pig.

"This is not reality. Why didn't you tell me I was to be the subject of an entertainment program where a gaggle of females were preselected to spend time with me in organized activities? Females I am not interested in. Why did you not tell me that I would be forced to spend time with them until I narrowed down the females to one to be my mate and receive my mating cuffs?" I asked that last, long question in one huge breath.

"Because you wouldn't have gone," Maxim said.

"Would you?" I countered, eyeing the Prillon governor. His brown hair was as dark as his mood. As leader of The Colony, he had a lot of responsibility and only seemed to smile when Rachel was about. He wasn't smiling now.

Good. He'd given permission for this mess.

"It was necessary, Wulf. The warriors here watch the broadcast as well. They are smiling. Laughing. They are excited on your behalf. There is hope."

Low blow. I could not let them down, and he knew it. Still I felt the need to warn him. "With all due respect, what if I fail? Would you want to be in my place?"

He shifted in his chair, his cheeks turning as bright a pink as mine probably were from the ridiculous amount of colored powder the frightened female had brushed onto my face. "No. Thankfully I already have a mate."

"I'm sure volunteers at the brides center must have increased. Let me end this. Get me the hell out of here. All I have to do is walk down to the transport room and I'll be gone."

"You can't!" Rachel practically shouted. "It has to go well, because what about the others? I mean, you're not the only one who's yet to be matched. And no, there has been no increase in brides, not yet. I think they are all watching, waiting to see how the show ends."

"Fuck."

She tried to smile, but I wasn't buying it. "Think of the females on Earth who will volunteer because they see you claiming a mate on their TVs. You are handsome and honorable. A human woman's dream. They're going to want a Wulf of their own."

I rolled my eyes. Gods be damned, I actually rolled my fucking eyes like a human.

"Then there's your fever," Maxim cautioned me.

As if I needed the reminder. My beast was always right below the surface, ready to break free, ready to stretch my skin, my bones, my size and take over.

I thought of all the fighters on The Colony who were waiting for a mate. Most had been tested by now, but the odds of being matched were slim. Only a small number had found mates, and all the females they'd been matched to were from Earth. Maxim was one of the lucky ones. Rachel, the mate he shared with Ryston, had volunteered to be tested and mated instead of facing a long prison sentence on her home planet. She was too fucking sweet and kind to have wallowed in a cell. She'd worked with Hunter Kiel's mate, a human woman named Lindsey, to devise this... scheme with some people within the Earth side of the Brides Program. It was the hope that this trip to Earth, that my public courting of these females, would grow the volunteer bride pool, which might mean matches for my friends. Rachel and Lindsey had good intentions, but I was the one paying the price.

Still, I couldn't let them down. Not the unmated warriors on The Colony, not Rachel nor Lindsey and not Governor Maxim, who had fought for every one of us at one time or another.

"I survived the Hive. I can finish this." I would control my beast with my last breath. I had no choice.

"That's the spirit!" Rachel pumped her fist in the air and

clapped Maxim on the shoulder. But his gaze did not lighten, and I knew he expected my next words.

"I have remained here and participated in this for the others. But Rachel, this episode is the last." I would see it through to the end, when I would kindly thank both females and take my leave like a male of honor, while I still could. Before I lost control. Because *my fever raged.*

"The grand finale!" She smiled and clapped her hands together. "I know. It's so exciting. I've been glued to the screen."

I frowned, having no idea what that meant.

"Seeing you in a tuxedo... wow, Wulf. You're hot."

I looked down at myself in this strange Earth outfit. With the shirt, something called a vest and a jacket, I *was* hot.

"Are you going to pick Genevieve or Willow?" she whispered as if I might share a secret.

I growled thinking of the two females my beast had disliked the least out of the twenty-four. I was not interested in mating either female. My beast had no desire to claim—or fuck—either of them. Admittedly they were beautiful women. Kind. Thoughtful. Eager to be matched. Eager to leave Earth. The mating fever was pushing me hard to find my mate, but neither of the finalists tempted my beast. Neither would be able to soothe him, let alone control him. A beast answered only to his mate. Without that feminine touch, we were lost.

It would be simple to choose one female on that stage. But my beast would not accept her as a mate, my fever would not be soothed and I would be forced to leave this planet before I hurt anyone when my beast raged and lost control. A false mate wasn't what my beast wanted, and admittedly neither did I. I wanted *her.* Whoever the fuck she was. The one to set my heart ablaze. My body, my cock would be perpetually hard for her. To be in her. To make her scream.

Genevieve and Willow didn't do any of that for me.

"I'm not going to pick either of them."

Her mouth fell open. "What?"

The lady with the brush had wrapped a small towel around my neck earlier, and the small paper cloth felt like it was choking me. Being here, my choices—or lack of them—was practically strangling me. Tugging the paper off, I threw it on a nearby desk. Fortunately the taping was being done at the testing center, since I wasn't officially allowed to wander around on the planet. They'd made a few exceptions... for dates. These... organized activities I had to do with the females, which were supposed to be fun. Romantic. I growled at the screen, hoping Maxim would take last-minute pity on me.

Yes, pity, and that proved how deep I'd sunk.

At least I was fortunate to be in a place with a comms station, offering me a direct connection to The Colony, to *home*. I'd been trying to talk Maxim, my governor, into intervening before the final episode, which was happening in just a few minutes.

"What?" Rachel said, her voice full of panic. "You have to pick one of them."

"Do you prefer either female to live on The Colony? I know you Earth ladies up there are close, but you'll have to include whoever I pick into your little group. Willow and Genevieve are fine females, but they won't be happy. Not with me. Especially since I'll have to fuck her for the rest of my life and my beast is livid at the possibility. He might refuse to touch her, to claim her. Females are meant to be treasured. Adored. I cannot do that. My beast refuses."

"It can't be that bad," Maxim said.

I eyed him for a moment. "My cock isn't rising for either of them. My beast would rather transport to Atlan and be executed. He would rather die. It is our way. The Atlan way."

Maxim cleared his throat at what was becoming a likelihood. My beast had been raging for a long time, the fever pushing me to find my mate. I knew it was part of the reason I'd been selected, hoping I'd find a female here in this... reality show... who was my mate. The alternative was death. That was looking more and more likely.

"Two minutes!" A perky female the size of an Atlan child stuck her head into the room, interrupting us, then disappeared.

Fuck.

"I've been on these things called dates with the females. I've gone on something called a fan boat in a water swamp to see prehistoric creatures with sharp teeth. I've walked along a beach barefoot. I've had something called a picnic. I've even gone swimming."

"At least you learned how from Mikki."

I growled and Rachel pinned her lips closed.

"I've done everything expected of me, including making twenty-two women cry at being rejected. I don't need to see an Earth sunset while holding hands with a female to know she, or any of them, are not my mate. I'm surprised females here don't demand to be tested to avoid such activities when they have no idea if the male they're spending time with is worthy."

"Preaching to the choir on that one," Rachel interjected. As I had no idea what she was talking about, I continued.

"A bride test is simple and quick and ensures they find the perfect mate." I sighed, knowing it wasn't the same on the males' side. I'd been tested years ago and even been matched. That had turned out to be a complete disaster. I'd been fighting the fever ever since, returned to space, to battle as an outlet for my rage. I had given the vast wealth and lands granted to me on Atlan to my family when I left for the second time. I had planned to go back, to try to find an Atlan female who would soothe me, but the Hive had killed that dream as well. Captured me. Tortured me. Turned me into... this.

I was out of time and out of options. My family on Atlan would be well taken care of. If I could convince even a handful of human females to be matched to others on The Colony, I could go to Atlan with a clear conscience. I would hold the beast back for one more day. One more night.

But I was glad I had an inner beast to let me know who my mate was—or *wasn't*. I could not hate him, nor regret that he was part of me. He had saved me in battle, killed countless enemies. He didn't deserve falsehood. He deserved respect. I would not force him to accept a female neither of us desired. If he preferred death, I would accept his choice.

"I must go."

"No, Wulf, listen! Just pick one. You can tell them the truth after the show," Rachel countered.

"My cuffs are in a glass case on the stage," I reminded her, pointing at the closed door and the stage that lay beyond. "They expect me to get down on a knee and offer the cuffs to one of them while the entire world watches." I took a step toward the screen and narrowed my eyes. "I'm Atlan. To make such an offer with no intent to claim the female would be dishonorable. My beast will not kneel for anyone but my true mate, Maxim."

The producer came through the door. He was a small human. Well, they were all small. His hair was gray, and he never seemed to stop talking. Or moving. I wanted to lift him up by the neck and tell him to fuck off. "Say goodbye to your space friends. This is a live show. We're live in thirty seconds. Now move!"

Yeah, I really wanted to finish him.

"Good luck. We'll be watching," Rachel said before the screen went dark.

2

Olivia Mercier, Interstellar Brides Program Testing Center, Backstage

I HEARD the alien's voice rumble through the walls and strained to make out what he was saying. Unfortunately the entire set was buzzing with excitement. Everyone was talking, rushing around like angry wasps under attack, moving cameras, checking mics, lighting. The fast-paced insanity of a live show had people amped like they had an IV of coffee direct into their veins.

"Makeup!" The yell from one of the show's producers had me scrambling.

It wasn't my name, but that was what I was called. Makeup. I was a faceless employee who did her job without being noticed.

"That's me. What do you need?" I asked the older gentleman who was frowning at one of the two women the Atlan warlord had chosen as his finalists. Her name was Genevieve, and she was beautiful. Really beautiful, with long blonde hair that fell in perfect waves to her waist, bright blue eyes lined expertly with traces of lavender and pink to bring out the color. She looked like a Miss America contestant... or a Barbie doll.

"Look at this. You tell me." The producer threw his hand in the general direction of Genevieve's face as she looked up at me helplessly. Her hands shook despite the fact that almost any single woman in the world would trade places with her in a heartbeat. I'd been watching the *Bachelor Beast* every night from home, and the Atlan warlord, Wulf?

God, he made my entire body wake up and pay attention. He was the chocolate sundae and the cherry on top.

I wanted one. The sundae, definitely, but a mate like Wulf.

But I would never qualify to be on a reality show like this, not that I'd tried. I was tall enough. That wasn't the problem. The problem was the extra weight I packed around my waist, my hips... hell, everywhere. I was not small. Both finalists could probably squeeze into the pants I was wearing—at the same time. I was called a *big girl*. Everywhere. Hell, I could probably fit both of Willow's ass cheeks in my damn bra.

A whiff of air left me at the comical thought. At least I had that on the skinny little thing. Genevieve had no cleavage. None. As much as I admired her supermodel-perfect body in every other way, I loved my big, heavy breasts. They were my best feature.

"Well?" the producer yelled, snapping me out of my usual rambling thoughts.

"What?" I asked him. "I think she looks amazing."

"Thanks, Olivia." Genevieve sat patiently, staring at the mirror in front of her seat at the makeup station. Neither one of us was going to win this argument, not when the producer was in one of these moods. Which was all day, every day.

"Those lips make her look like a stripper. Give her a pale pink. Something natural. We're selling true love here. She's not pole dancing." With that, he stormed off to scream at his next victim.

With an apologetic wince, I reached for the makeup remover cloths. "Sorry. I'll have to wipe it off and start over."

Genevieve sighed. "That's all right." She leaned back and tilted her head up so I could have easier access. "I liked the hot pink."

"Me, too." It was the truth. With her fair coloring, the bright pink not only matched the shade I'd used on her eyelids, but her blush, too, and made her lips pop.

I'd done my best to make the final two contestants look gorgeous. Which wasn't hard, considering they both appeared like they'd stepped off a runway in Paris wearing formal evening gowns. Genevieve's dress was a dark navy, as the producers felt black was morbid, but they wanted to contrast with her blonde hair and fair skin. The other contestant, Willow, was a black-haired goddess. I didn't know if she was mixed race, Italian, Hispanic or Asian. She was exotic looking. Black hair, almond-shaped eyes, rich, dark skin. Her gown was ivory. The jewels around her neck perfectly matched the amber tone of her eyes. The two finalists were darkness and light standing next to each other. Too beautiful to be real.

It was exactly what I thought about the alien who was the star of the show. Seven feet tall if he was an inch, his shoulders were twice the size of mine and his hands were as big as dinner plates. I'd watched as he ducked as he went through doorways. Every talk show and media outlet in the world had been speculating about this mysterious "Beast" he turned.

He wasn't just a guy from another planet; he was a veteran. He'd fought the mysterious and dangerous Hive, even been captured by them and somehow escaped. He was like a movie hero, not a reality show hunk.

That beast? It came out not only in danger, but to claim a mate as well. A gorgeous female and the tantalizing prospect of beast sex? It was like the "Beauty and the Beast" fairy tale come to life. The rated R version. Maybe triple X if his cock was as big as the rest of him.

I wanted to fan myself at how hot that thought was.

Wulf, being Wulf, was one reason the entire *world* was watching the grand finale tonight, broadcast live in a few minutes.

It was also the reason I'd been over the moon when Lucy had offered to babysit for me so I could stay and watch the show. She and I had been on the makeup crew since the beginning, when there had been twenty-four women to get ready. I'd never seen the beast—the Atlan— in real life. My job was the ladies' makeup, and that had kept me here in this room, making them all gorgeous. Now, with only two remaining, just a few of us were needed. Lucy and I had traded tonight, and I was so excited to see what happened. Right in front of me. Live. I wanted to see Wulf once before he picked his mate and transported back to The Colony.

Wulf never came in until the last minute, and I was always gone by then, off the clock and forced to watch the latest episode from my couch like everyone else in the world.

Lucy said he was even *more* gorgeous in real life, which didn't seem possible. Even through my television screen, he was... there were no words. Virile. Handsome. Rugged. Wild. Feral. Untamed. Controlled. Potent.

"Two minutes!" The stage crew was yelling, and everyone scrambled into position as I swiped the last touches of a neutral pink onto Genevieve's lips. She was still beautiful. Stunning, really. I hoped she would get a happily ever after.

Someone should, and it wasn't going to be me.

"Where are my girls? Willow. Good. Right there." There was a pause, and we both tensed even before the stage manager was shouting at the top of her lungs. "Genevieve? Get out here! Twenty seconds!"

Genevieve slipped off the makeup chair with a nervous smile. Even her lips were shaking.

"Break a leg," I whispered, squeezing her hand. "You'll be great."

"Thanks." She hurried into position, and I followed until I stood in the darkest shadow of the set I could find, stage right, as the music began and the announcer, an arrogant asshole named Chet Bosworth—*Really? Chet freaking Bosworth?*—came into view with his fake teeth, fake smile, and more makeup on his face than the women. Not that he needed it. He was one of the beautiful people, too.

He *did* have several million followers on social media, most of them panting women, so I rolled my eyes as he tilted his hip and winked at the camera.

"Hello out there and welcome back to the exciting finale of the *Bachelor Beast*. Tonight our world, or universe famous"—he chuckled at his own joke—"and very eligible bachelor, Warlord Wulf, an Atlan currently stationed on The Colony planet, will *finally* choose his bride."

The lights flickered, cueing the live audience to stomp and clap, which they did with great enthusiasm. I did, too.

"From twenty-four eligible mates, Wulf has narrowed the field to the final two single women standing on this stage. Both beautiful, intelligent and very eager to be his bride. Who will he choose? Who will his beast claim? Which one of these lovely ladies will be offered the prize, not only of the priceless alien mating cuffs, but the unwavering devotion of an Atlan's beast?" The crowd went wild again, and even my heart rate, already practically pounding out of my chest in excitement, kicked up a notch. He was good at his job, big-toothed Chet Bosworth. "Do you want to know?"

The ladies in the audience screamed, and I clapped twice before I caught myself. With a flourish of his wrist, he whirled around and the curtains that had been hiding the final contestants opened to reveal Genevieve and Willow, both with dazzling, if nervous, smiles on their faces.

Chet winked again at the camera. "Who will the Atlan beast choose? It's time to find out."

Chet kept talking to build up tension—as if people around the globe weren't on the edge of their seats—while a murmur moved through the crew backstage. I knew the Atlan would come from stage left, and I'd positioned myself to get the best view possible while remaining unseen. The producer didn't mind if the crew watched the show, in fact, demanded it, in case of a makeup or hair emergency or wardrobe malfunction. But there were only two women onstage tonight, and I wasn't responsible for the Atlan's makeup.

Confident in my skills, I knew the ladies wouldn't need me. Which left me free to watch... and forget to breathe.

There he was. Warlord Wulf. God help me, he was huge. I'd seen him on the television screen, but that had been a pale comparison to the raw sexual magnetism pouring off the alien in waves so thick I felt like I was choking. My dormant hormones screamed at me to *wake the fuck up* as he stomped his way out of camera view on stage left.

They'd put the alien in a very human tuxedo, and the black material hugged him like a second skin. He was all muscles. Pure, bulging power. He had to weigh close to three hundred pounds, but there couldn't be an ounce of fat on him. His expression was serious, unhappy. He looked uncomfortable, as if the tuxedo was strangling him.

"Oh shit." I whispered the words before I could stop myself. I had never once considered the fact that the Atlan alien didn't want to be here. But clearly he was not happy. Surely he'd find happiness with Genevieve or Willow. I'd seen the earlier episodes. He was reserved in his actions and his emotions. Quiet. Calm. I'd thought he'd been told by the producer not to give away too much while filming, but now? I wasn't so sure.

Both ladies were barely holding it together. Shaking. Hugging each other like the last two women in an international beauty pageant, waiting to discover who would get the crown.

This man? Alien. Whatever. He was a god on two feet. Any woman he chose would feel like a queen.

"Tonight Warlord Wulf will finally choose his bride. Per Atlan custom, he will kneel before her and ask her to accept his mating cuffs. For those of you out there wondering what those are, let's take a look at the stunning artistry of his traditional bracelets that have come all the way from planet Atlan."

Chet Bosworth walked over to a large glass case where two sets of what looked like wide bracelets lay side by side under the glass, on display like Cinderella's glass slipper.

Two large and two small. Two for him, and two smaller ones for his bride to wear around her wrists.

I had to admit, it was romantic.

The cuffs were beautiful. I'd sneaked a peek when I first arrived and been told that they were handmade by craftsmen on Atlan and each family had a unique design. The cuffs on display represented Wulf's family heritage, the delicate and stunning weaving of dark gray and silver fancier than the most elaborate Celtic designs I'd seen. They were beautiful, the Atlan version of wedding rings, but they served another purpose. A visible claiming.

Warlord Wulf was flat out scowling as Chet leaned over and the cameraman zoomed in close to show the people at home exactly what the cuffs looked like. They did this every night, and I knew what was seen at home. I'd also heard Chet's annoying and faux scandalized voice explain why the Atlans presented the cuffs to their female mate.

"As you all know, folks, Warlord Wulf is suffering from a common Atlan affliction known as mating fever. The Atlan males all carry, buried within them, a beast capable of rending and tearing, of destroying enemies on the field of battle. But once they reach a certain age, they are no longer able to control their wild side alone. They need the delicate touch of a female, a mate—a bride—to tame their, shall we say, beastly desires?"

His conspiratorial chuckle made me want to slap him. God, he was annoying and dramatic.

Narcissists the world over would be proud.

"If Warlord Wulf does not choose a bride tonight, I have been told—and this is new, folks..." Chet stood and indicated the cameraman should span back and focus on his and the contestants' reactions to his next words. "He will be sent back to Atlan and—"

Genevieve and Willow looked at each other, confused.

This *was* new. The ladies couldn't fake this, which meant they'd held back on all of us. Typical.

I looked at Warlord Wulf, who stood in the shadows, waiting to come onstage when he was cued, but his hands were in fists and he closed his eyes as if fighting for control.

Holy shit.

"I can't. I can't believe this, folks."

Chet, a true master at the art of dramatics, waited until the audience was making enough unsettled noise to be heard at home. "If Warlord Wulf does not claim a bride tonight, now, in just a few moments, he will be sent back to Atlan and he. Will. Be. Put. To. Death!"

I gasped, along with everyone else. That couldn't be true. Could it?

Glancing at the most beautiful man I'd ever seen—and the biggest—I didn't see shock or denial on his face. I saw... acceptance at what Chet had said. Oh God.

No. Just no.

He *had* to choose a bride. That was it. *Had to.* Or die.

Chet's flair for the dramatics was, for once, true.

Genevieve was beautiful. Nice enough. She'd always been pleasant to me. Willow was a bit more extroverted, but I liked her as well. They were both genuine women hoping for true love. Surely he could pick one and avoid... execution.

I thought dating on Earth sucked. The poor Atlan across from me took things to a whole new level. Find your special someone or be put to death? That seemed a bit extreme.

God, what a waste. He was so damn perfect, so gorgeous. So... sexy.

"Now, before we bring the bachelor of the hour out onstage, let's take a look back over how these two beautiful women made the final cut and earned a chance to be claimed by the Bachelor Beast." He winked at the camera. "Right after this short message from our sponsors."

"Aaaaaand we're out." The director yelled the all clear, and the room burst into chaos as everyone discussed the newest revelation. I stood quietly, hidden, and watched the alien stand still as stone, waiting.

The commercial break dragged on for several minutes as the producers milked the show for every advertising dollar possible. The entire time Wulf stood still as a statue. Unmoving.

I ached to run across the stage and give him a hug, but he had no idea who I was. It would be damn awkward, to say the least.

Hi, big guy. You don't know me, but I feel sorry for you and want to give you a hug.

I did feel bad for him. But at least he had two of the most beautiful women I'd ever seen to choose from. He wouldn't die. He would live a fantasy life on The Colony with one of the lovely creatures onstage.

I'd go home, grateful that my dating dry spell didn't come with planet Atlan–level consequences.

The stage manager cued the audience and Chet that the show was back, and the techies played the promised videos. Even I couldn't tear my gaze from the large screens mounted above the stage as they showed a compilation of video clips of first Genevieve, then Willow on various dates with Wulf. Just as I'd remembered, he was always courteous. Respectful. Polite. There was even an interview clip where Willow had complained that she'd tried to put the moves on him and he'd turned her down.

Like what was that about? He was obviously a male in his prime. He'd chosen her over and over, episode after episode. Her and Genevieve. So why not go for it when she was so obviously willing? Why not soothe that beast? It made no sense.

Every man I knew would have taken her offer and had her naked immediately.

So, what? He was a warrior and a monk? Did they have some kind of celibacy rule? Wulf was sex on a stick, a walking orgasm. No way he didn't have women throwing themselves at him on The Colony. He had to be what? Thirty? Forty? It was hard to tell with an alien. He was full-grown and made my pussy clench with things I hadn't dared feel in a long damn time.

Too long.

But then I'd had a lot to deal with the last few months. Sex with an Atlan beast wasn't one of them. Any guy for that matter. Okay, maybe when I lay in bed at night, I thought about Wulf and what it would be like to be with him, but I was the ugly duckling in comparison to the two swans onstage, Genevieve and Willow.

It wasn't only my average looks and curvy figure holding me back. The fact was, my life was a Dumpster fire. Tears welled up, and I lost focus on the show. On Chet's rambling.

No. I wasn't going to think about what my life had become or the responsibilities I'd inherited from my dead brother, and I wasn't talking about Tanner and Emma. Not now. Right this minute I was going to ogle the eye candy who'd just been introduced and dream that he liked big girls with curves, lots and lots of curves, instead of supermodels with perfect pink lipstick.

"We're back on the *Bachelor Beast*," Chet said, grinning at the camera. "Let's bring out the alien of the hour, Warlord Wulf!"

The audience went wild as Wulf walked onstage. His gait

was swift and ate up the space in only a few steps. His hands were clenched into fists at his sides as he stopped in front of his chair as if he were a puppet being moved by strings and not a warlord who'd survived the Hive. It had been especially made for his supersized frame, huge and sturdy. His gaze shifted to Genevieve and Willow, and he offered them a respectful nod. Nothing more.

Chet walked over to Wulf. Their size difference was impressive as both men stood on the raised platform. I'd seen reruns of *The Dating Game* from the seventies, and this set had a similar feel with orange carpet and a white lattice backdrop. It only made Chet look more ridiculous and Wulf more... just more.

What woman would want an Earth man after knowing that Wulf wasn't the only Atlan out there? He'd choose Genevieve or Willow, but he was here to promote the Interstellar Brides Program, where any volunteer could get a perfectly matched mate of her own.

I'd considered taking the matching test but learned that I didn't meet the qualifications since I was the guardian of my niece and nephew. While I hadn't given birth to them, they were legally mine, and I couldn't leave them here on Earth for a hot alien match. No. Tanner and Emma were everything to me. I didn't need a man if it meant giving them up. Never.

"Let's look back on the warlord's time here on Earth," Chet said.

The light on the camera went out, and I knew prerecorded and edited footage was being shown to the home audience. Chet tipped his head back to look up at Wulf. "Have a seat," he told him, his arm out, indicating where Wulf should go. As if it wasn't obvious.

Wulf didn't say a word as he dropped into the white

leather seat that looked a whole lot like a huge throne. Now Chet was taller, which was obviously his sole reason for the request. His ego was wider than Wulf's shoulders.

I took a step closer, careful of the thick cords across the floor while remaining behind the cameras. Wulf's hands gripped the arms of his chair as if they were keeping him from flying away. Maybe because I looked at people's faces all the time, I could often tell what they were feeling, or maybe Wulf was equally bad at hiding his emotions.

I'd lusted after him. Drooled over him. Dreamed of him. I hadn't really thought of the toll this show was taking on him. Had he truly volunteered for this? He looked about as enthused to be sitting here as someone in the waiting room before a colonoscopy. Was what Chet had said true? Would he die if he didn't pick Genevieve or Willow? Was he really going to be executed?

Was his life so bad that he'd choose execution over the women? Not once in the three weeks of taping had Chet asked him what he was looking for in a mate. Everyone assumed, including me, that Wulf was whittling down the ladies to his favorites, to the one he'd give his cuffs.

Now I wasn't so sure.

The show dragged on, as they had a one-hour time slot, with plenty of commercial breaks to heighten the anticipation. I was ready to scream by the time Chet stopped his inane questions and finally got down to the business at hand. The choice. Wulf's choice.

"It's finally time. Genevieve, Willow..." Chet spoke and the ladies took a step closer. The lights dimmed except for a focused beam on the gleaming cuffs in the glass case.

I moved around another camera to be as close as I could but remain behind the scenes. We were all in shadows, the large set being lit only by the stage.

"Warlord Wulf. It is time."

Wulf slowly rose to his feet.

"Who is going to be your bride? Genevieve or Willow?"

Mary, a wardrobe tech, moved to stand beside me but bumped my shoulder, pushing me forward. I gasped and stopped my forward momentum out of sheer panic. I didn't get in the way, but my heart was in my throat. Mary's hand settled on my shoulder, and she mouthed a *sorry* along with a small smile.

I looked back at the stage, at what I'd been waiting for since the first episode. But Wulf wasn't looking at the final contestants. He was looking at me.

Me.

Oh. My. God.

Had I gotten in front of the camera? Had I distracted Wulf at a time like this? Oh shit, I was going to be fired. I took a small step back, but Mary stopped me.

Genevieve turned to look my way. Willow narrowed her eyes in my direction as if trying to peer into the shadows. Chet even broke his perfect facade to glance past the cameras.

At me. Although I wasn't sure if they could actually see me, or if they were trying to determine what held Wulf's attention.

A rumbling came from the stage. Chet, Genevieve and Willow whipped their gazes back toward Wulf. Then came a growl that practically made the floor shake. I felt it deep inside me and I gasped.

Wulf's eyes were still on me, and I couldn't look away. Not when he was growing. Actually growing. The audience gasped, murmured. Backstage whispering kicked in. Chet stepped back. Genevieve took hold of Willow's hand, and their eyes widened.

The tuxedo jacket ripped at the seams on Wulf's body. He wasn't seven feet of alien any longer. He had to be eight feet and all beast. Angled features, ragged breathing, taut muscles. A gaze laser sharp. Intense, as if he was ready to pounce.

"Mine." The one word was low and deep, and it silenced the entire set.

Wulf's arm went out, and he moved Chet out of the way as if he were a puppet. With his heel, he backkicked the throne chair, and it went flying across the stage and into the lattice backdrop.

It broke and part of it clattered to the stage.

Shrieks filled the air, and audience members began to panic, having no idea what Wulf was going to do. They'd taunted the beast for three weeks, and now everyone was surprised when it appeared.

I had to admit I was panicked, too, but I couldn't move. I could only watch.

Wulf stalked across the stage.

"Um, makeup girl... he's looking at you," Mary said, fear in her voice.

"No way. He's looking at you," I countered. Makeup girl. Yep. No one in this place knew my name. Invisible. As always. Except, apparently, right freaking now.

She took a step to the left, out of the beast's path. Wulf's gaze did not follow her. "No, it's you."

Oh shit. He *was* staring at me.

"Ladies and gentleman, it seems there's been a change in plans. It appears Warlord Wulf's beast has chosen to make an appearance. We're live on set, and as you can see, he's grown impossibly larger. If I hadn't witnessed this for myself, I wouldn't believe it. It seems his beast has seen something offstage and will not be deterred from reaching it."

"Mine."

Chet sputtered. I felt like a doe in the headlights.

This couldn't be what I thought it was. This huge, gorgeous alien man was *not* talking about me. No freaking way.

I took a step backward.

Wulf's roar made people scream.

I didn't scream. I couldn't breathe.

Chet had his dramatic voice back under control. "Ladies and gentlemen, what we are seeing is unprecedented in the history of live television. It appears that the alien, Warlord Wulf, has decided to choose a member of our audience as his mate."

Wulf spun around and faced Chet. The man turned pale under his thick stage makeup. When Wulf loomed over him, Chet gulped, his Adam's apple bobbing. Wulf grabbed the microphone out of Chet's hand and squeezed, crumpling the metal as if it were tinfoil, then dropped it to the orange carpet.

Wulf turned around, ignored Chet entirely and made his way in my direction again.

"Turn the cameras!" the producer hissed.

The one nearest me swung about, and I was about to jump out of the way of its path when Wulf stopped it with his palm. The cameraman retreated to safety, and with one push Wulf toppled the huge machine onto its side. The crash reverberated through the set, but all I heard was a second, "Mine," coming from Wulf's lips. The producer screamed at the other cameras to get the shot as Wulf stopped directly before me and... sniffed.

I looked up. Way up. My head was tilted so far back my

chin was facing him more than my eyes. My mouth hung open.

"Um... hi."

"Mate."

"Uh... no. No, no. No," I stuttered.

"Mine."

Taking another deep breath, he growled. Men with handheld cameras surrounded us, absorbing in everything. What was I wearing? God, I had on my white T-shirt with the word *sassy* in sequins across my chest. It was almost laundry day, and I wore a skirt I'd found in the back of my closet. My hair was up in a sloppy bun, and while I did makeup for a living, I wore none. Holy crap, I was on live TV around the world.

I couldn't think of that now. An Atlan warlord was looming over me, breathing hard and saying *mine.*

"Genevieve or Willow are lovely choices for a mate. You should pick one of them," I said, my voice shaky.

"No. You. Mate."

My eyes widened and I stared. You could have heard a pin drop on the set... and Wulf's ragged breathing.

"Me?" I set a hand on my chest, and his gaze dropped. Kept moving down, all the way to my feet, then back up to my face. His gaze was focused, unblinking.

"You."

"This is a new twist, ladies and gentleman," Chet stage-whispered. "It appears our Atlan beast has surprised everyone and chosen his mate. But she's not a contestant. She is an employee of the studio production team, a makeup artist, if I am correct?" He looked to the producer for confirmation, and I wanted to slap the idiot.

"We know nothing about her, folks. Is she married? Does she have children? A boyfriend?" The last was said with a conspiratorial chuckle. "Our big Atlan beast wouldn't be too pleased with that turn of events, would he?"

Wulf turned his head in Chet's direction, glared until Chet lost his cheeky smile, then looked around at the crowd of very interested people.

Before I could even blink, Wulf scooped me up in his arms as if I really was his bride, and walked off. Yup, walked right past the backstage people, past Chet Bosworth, who was saying something frantically, and to the door that led to the backstage area.

"Wait. I... you..."

"Mine. Mate. You."

I shook my head, but all I could think about was how strong he was, the feel of his muscles as he held me against him. How big he was. How far off the ground he held me. How hot his chest was, like he had a... fever.

Oh my God. This alien giant thought I was his mate.

My body wasn't arguing. Reality, however, wasn't going to play nice. I could not be mated to an alien. Could. Not. No matter how magnificent he was.

This simply was *not* going to work.

3

THE SECOND THE door of his makeshift dressing room slammed closed behind him, Wulf turned and pressed my back against it. He shifted me as if I weighed less than a feather so our eyes were level. He stared and stared.

I stared right back because he was inches away. All perfect, frantic alien and I was in his arms. Caught by his dark gaze.

"Mine."

His eyes said he was deadly serious, and no matter what the handful of working brain cells I had left said to me, I couldn't look away. I didn't *want* to look away. I had never had a man, any man, look at me like he was now.

Like I was beautiful. Perfect. Desired.

Jeez, I really was in over my head here. Things had gone a little crazy in the past two minutes.

"You should... you should probably put me down so I

can get back to work." Not that I had been working, but what was I supposed to say? I had felt almost sorry for him while I'd been watching him prepare to go onstage, but now I didn't know what to think. Maybe he *had* gone crazy, because he seemed to be choosing me over the two pageant-queen hotties.

His eyes narrowed, but I wasn't scared. Surprised, definitely. No, stunned. Holy crap. But not scared. "Really. I should go. I am going to get fired."

"No. Stay. Mine." The beast inside him was having none of it as he used one leg to prop me up—that hard thigh right between my legs and pressing against my center—as he moved those large hands to my sides. Every touch made me burn, like he was contagious, like this mating fever he had was infecting me.

One of his hands slid along the outer edge of my breast and down my side to cup my ass. I groaned, my eyes closing before I could stop myself. It had been too long since I'd been with anyone, and not one lover had ever touched me like this. Like I was soft and vulnerable and precious. "You should stop. You made a mistake. I'm no one."

"Mate. Mine."

My eyes flew open, realizing he was saying the same thing over and over. He wasn't romantic. This wasn't candlelight and roses. This was intense. This was possessiveness to the extreme. He'd practically kidnapped me. Damned if that fact didn't make me all hot and melty. But I was a realist. This... obsession his beast seemed to have in me was wrong. Maybe it was my shampoo, a scent that was drawing him that his real mate had. "I'm... not."

I kinda wanted to be, 'cause what girl didn't want this kind of attention?

My resistance made him growl, and I felt the vibrations move from his chest and into mine.

"Name." It wasn't a question but a demand, and I'd heard enough about these Atlan beasts on the gossip sites to know he couldn't really say full sentences, not while his beast was in control. Maybe the special translation brain chip I'd heard everyone in space got was broken. I clearly remembered Chet stating in the first episode that Wulf had been chosen as the first bachelor beast because of his ability to speak English. He could understand it fluently because of the processor he had in his head, but it didn't give him the ability to speak very well. He had to *know* the language to do that. He was no dummy. Chet talked everyone up to make the show more fanciful and exotic, but I had no idea how to speak Atlan and I wasn't savvy enough to take a class and be able to go to the planet and be a contestant on a reality show.

God, I'd never thought of that before, how hard it must be for him to be here. Now, with his beast all focused and growly and a little crazy? No wonder he was monosyllabic.

I licked my lips, and his piercing gaze followed the action. This close, I saw how dark his eyes were, how strong his jaw, the stark line of his nose, strong brow. Every inch of him was... more. As if human guys were wimps.

"I'm Olivia. Olivia Mercier." I thought of Genevieve and Willow. The episodes all showed them talking and Wulf listening. I'd thought him quiet. Introverted. How had the two finalists gotten to know him when he'd rarely spoken?

"You have mate?"

This time it *was* a question, and I answered with the truth before I realized I'd blown my one chance to make sure he would let me go. "No. I'm single."

The rumble in his chest said that information pleased

him, and he lowered his nose to my neck, breathed deeply. I shivered. Oh. My. God.

"Mine."

Was he ever planning on letting me down? My feet had to be two feet off the floor. The door was hard at my back, but he was equally solid against my front. I wasn't going anywhere unless he decided it.

"Listen, Wulf." I squirmed, placing my hands on his shoulders. *God, the freaking muscles.* With the half-ripped tuxedo dangling from his shoulders in tatters from when he'd shifted to his beast, my fingertips made contact with skin. Hot, soft skin that I really, really wanted to explore. *Get a grip, Olivia.*

"There has been some kind of mistake."

"Mate." His lips caressed the side of my neck, and I would have swooned if I'd been on my feet. Which I wasn't. It was getting very hard to concentrate. He smelled like hot sex. Like alpha male. Like heat and skin and something I knew was just *him.*

My body was responding to him as if it had a mind of its own. Or an inner girl beast. At least an inner nymphomaniac because I liked being manhandled by him. I was securely where he wanted me, but I wasn't being hurt. I had a feeling it would upset him if he injured me somehow.

I was trying to think of something intelligent to say when he lifted me in his arms and carried me over to a high-backed chair nearly identical to the throne-like monstrosity he'd kicked through the back wall of the set. It was against a wall out of the way, as if it were in reserve in case the first one broke. Well, the first one did break, but that was kind of irrelevant now.

I thought he would sit down and place me in his lap, but no. He settled my ass all the way on top of the high back.

"Um... Wulf?"

My spot was barely wide enough to hold me without being uncomfortable. I felt like a doll propped up on a shelf, but I was far from doll-like. If I slid forward off the edge, I'd land several feet down and probably bounce off the chair's comfy seat.

He placed his hand on my chest, just below my neck. Gently he pushed me until my back was against the wall. This was crazy! I was sitting on the top of his high-back chair, legs open, my pussy *right there* in front of his face. I was *that* high up. I was wearing my laundry day skirt, which rode *way* up my thighs.

"Um, Wulf." This couldn't be happening. Was this happening? What was he going to do? Was I going to let this happen?

His hands came to rest on my thighs, and he pushed my skirt higher, higher.

Oh shit. I think so. Yes. No. Maybe?

Even though there was the seat of the chair between us, he was so big that he could lean forward and... he breathed me in. I was wet. I knew he would smell it. "Oh God."

Wait, what panties was I wearing? And my thighs... I could see the dimples on them from here.

"Wulf." That wasn't a deterrent.

Dipping his head, he placed his lips on the inside of my thigh, right over those ripples of thick flesh, kissing both legs in turn, over and over. He didn't seem to notice I wasn't supermodel fit. In fact, he didn't seem to notice one specific part of me other than my pussy.

"I taste now."

I taste now. Holy shit. I tensed, not knowing what to expect. Okay, I knew what to expect... but with him? Where I was sitting? Someone could come in at any time. In fact, I was surprised no one had, that there wasn't a camera zoomed in on Wulf's face as it hovered over my laundry-day panty-covered pussy.

Yet, through all that panic, it was so fucking hot I had no idea what to say or do.

But he stopped, looked up at me. "Taste. Yes?"

He was asking permission. Damn and double damn. Did I want his mouth on me? There?

I nodded and bit my lip. "But... others..." I looked away from him and at the door.

"Locked."

I had no idea when he'd locked it, but I had to guess when he had me pressed up against it. "Then, yes."

A thousand times yes. This wasn't a Jane Austen book, but I could totally relate to Jane Bennet in the heat of the moment.

His smile was feral and a little wild as he reached up my skirt and ripped the thong underwear open with one finger and let them drop to the seat of the huge chair. They were plain black, but it didn't seem an Atlan beast cared about panties.

Wulf pushed my skirt up to my hips and kissed his way along my thighs. Then his mouth was on me, sucking and tasting. I arched my neck, my back bowed and I grabbed at the wall behind me in a futile attempt to find something to hold on to. There was nothing but him, his head, the dark strands of his hair caught in my fingers as I whimpered and opened my legs farther.

He fucked me with his tongue and I nearly exploded, but it wasn't enough. Not quite enough. I needed more...

"Ahhh!"

Wulf replaced his tongue with two fingers. Two *big* fingers worked me open, fucking me deep as his tongue worked my clit. I never came easily with a guy, making me wonder if I was defective. Now I knew I hadn't had the right guy, because I didn't last long, the pleasure so intense. His scent was like a drug, his heat wrapping around me like a safety net, his strength the ultimate temptation for a woman who'd been struggling on her own for too damn long. And that tongue... those fingers. Wicked. Ruthless. Unrelenting.

I wanted to give in. I felt... feminine. Sexy. Desirable. Safe.

He flicked his tongue once. Twice. Sucked my clit into his mouth. Fucked me with his fingers.

I exploded, shudders racking my body while pushing me to go higher, working me further as the orgasm rode me hard.

"Wulf." His name left my mouth, and I didn't know what I wanted to say. Thank you? Stop? More? Mostly I wished this fantasy moment could last forever.

"Mine."

He pulled back and I sighed in regret at his loss, but then I was being lifted and turned, my back against the door once more, the cold, hard surface a shock to my warm, dazed existence. I heard the sound of a belt buckle, the slide of a zipper.

"Wulf," I repeated, looking up at the popcorn texture of the ceiling. My blood was humming through my veins, my muscles like pulled taffy.

I felt the prod of him then, the rock-hard tip of an enormous cock at the entrance of my wet core. My inner walls clenched with anticipation of being filled. His fingers were one thing, but the heat from just the tip of his cock... I sighed.

"Mate. Fuck now." He held perfectly still, again waiting for my permission to slide into my body and make me come once more. I was close, the first orgasm feeling like a warm-up. I wanted more. I'd taken birth control pills since I was thirteen to regulate my period. I wasn't going to get pregnant. I was going to break every rule I'd ever had for myself when it came to men and dating. Never have sex on the first date—and this wasn't even a date. Never go out with someone I didn't know for at least two months. Never…

Yet here I was, up against a door with an alien's cock ready to sink into my pussy. I felt like I'd slipped into an alternate reality. Was this a dream? Was a gorgeous Atlan wanting to fuck *me*? Sure, this was a quickie. We were in a random room backstage, after all. But he hadn't pulled off my panties and fucked me. No, he'd used his mouth on me first. Got me off. A mouth that glistened with my wetness even now.

He growled and shifted, the tip of him rubbing against my clit, moving slowly back and forth across my pussy. Fuck me, that was hot. How could I say no? My body didn't want to. It wanted an alien cock stretching me open and making me come. I owed it to the women of Earth, didn't I?

Screw that, I owed it to myself. I'd been good my whole dang life, and it had gotten me in a shit-ton of problems. I owed money to a fucking drug dealer because of my dumbass dead brother. I'd been good, but my brother had been a holy terror and I was the one that got the shaft.

Well, I wanted a different kind of shaft now. Hard. Deep. "Yes."

His entire body shuddered as he settled me over him. He was huge, my pussy spreading slowly to take him in, the stretch bordering on pain.

Someone pounded on the door, and I felt it against my back. It was background noise. Nothing more. My entire being was focused on Wulf. On his heat. His body pressed against mine. The scent of his chest in front of my face. The huge cock filling me to the breaking point.

He was all the way inside me, or at least all of him that I could take. My inner walls rippled, and I wiggled my hips to adjust. Our eyes met. Held. There, I saw heat. Need. This was where he wanted to be. Inside me.

"Weeks. This. Need." Tendons in his neck were taut, his hands on my ass held me up as his hips rolled and he began to fuck me.

I understood him. He'd needed this, to fuck me, ever since he got here. He'd had to deal with the show and the women, but it seemed they hadn't appealed to him. He'd craved a connection like this, but he hadn't found it with any of them.

He found it with me.

"Warlord, open the door!"

"Olivia, are you all right?"

More pounding, more shouting, but Wulf paid them no attention.

"The door's locked. Someone find a fucking key."

I didn't last. This was sex unlike anything I'd ever imagined. Better than any random porn clip I'd seen on the Internet. Only a few inches of metal door separated porn-worthy sex from the rest of the world. I was the star of the show, the hot, sexy woman who was being fucked against the door by the sexiest, most virile alpha male anyone on this planet had ever seen.

Me. Chubby since elementary school, three boyfriends my entire life, me.

He was pumping into me like he couldn't stop, like he needed me more than he needed air to breathe. Like I was a goddess. A sex goddess.

The feel of his cock rubbing over places deep inside me,

the heat moving from his body into mine. The raggedness of his breath. The way he watched me, as if ensuring every shift of his cock was for my benefit.

"Wulf," I said again, gripping his shoulders.

"Mate," he countered.

I heard the jiggle of the door handle, the slight push of the door. Wulf only leaned in more, ensuring it wasn't going to open.

"Mine," he snarled as he pulled almost out and slammed back in.

I cried out.

"He's hurting her! Get the police."

"He's a beast... what are they going to do?"

Conversations on the other side of the door swirled around me, but it was Wulf and only Wulf I paid attention to. He wasn't going to hurt me. He was going to make me feel better than I'd ever felt in my entire life. His hand was on the door, holding it closed.

No one was going to get past him. No one. He was mine right now, and I was his. The thought pushed me closer to the edge.

"I'm going to come," I told him.

"Yes." He altered the angle of his thrust again, and he pressed against my clit.

Colors danced behind my closed eyelids as I came, milking his cock, wanting him deeper, hoping to feel like this forever. "Wulf," I cried.

I felt a growl reverberate through his chest as he took me hard, flesh slapping.

"Mine. Mine. Mine," he said with each deep thrust until he held himself inside, his fingers clenching my ass as he came.

I felt the heat of it fill me. I looked at him, watched him

as he found his pleasure in my body. I made him like this. Wild. Feral. Sated.

Not one of the twenty-four gorgeous women had made him this way. No one but me saw him like this. Vulnerable. Lost. Perfect.

"Warlord Wulf. You must open this door now. We have sent for guards to stun you."

Wulf didn't even move, so I had to assume the threat— from a guy who sounded like the producer—didn't bother him.

"Wulf, we have to let them in," I said, stroking his sweaty hair back from his face. He was still hard inside me, but I felt his cum seep out.

It was over. *This* was over, whatever it was. One time. One wild, incredible time.

"No."

I waited until he looked at me again. "We can't stay in here forever. The show was ruined. We have to face them."

I was most likely out of a job. Fuck.

Carefully he pulled out and lowered me to my feet and set one hand on the door by my head to keep it closed. He was that strong.

Now his muscles weren't as tense. His gaze not as fierce. Fucking had soothed him a bit. I couldn't blame him. Two orgasms and I was ready for a huge nap. But I had alien cum sliding down the insides of my thighs and my employers banging down the door at my back.

I also had one final drop to make for that asshole, Jimmy, before I could go to sleep tonight. "We have to open the door."

He nodded, then helped me work my skirt down, ensuring I was completely put back together, minus the panties. With one hand he tucked himself back in his tuxedo pants, and I helped him with the zipper and belt buckle. It was an intimate act, and we did it in silence.

Only when we dressed—not that it was going to be hard for anyone to miss what we'd been up to—did he pull me out of the way of the door, then open it.

People surrounded us, shouting. I was tugged away from Wulf as guys with cameras on their shoulders got in my face and as close to Wulf as they dared. Questions were shouted, and I didn't know where to look. What to say. I was pushed through the doorway and into the hall and caught a glimpse of Wulf as he moved to get closer to me.

This was insanity. I was no one. A quick fuck for an out-of-control alien. When Genevieve and Willow were pushed into the dressing room to stand with Wulf, I knew this little fling was over. The cameras were still rolling. Chet the Magnificent had found a new microphone, of course.

Had this been a big prank? Had they planned this all along? For ratings? For shock value? Had it been real or part of the media circus that followed Wulf around like bees after pollen? Had he been in on it?

Did it matter? I had to get home, get changed and do the only thing I could to keep the people I loved safe. I didn't have time to figure this out right now. I definitely didn't want to try to figure it out on live television.

And there, looking flustered but eyes flashing with excitement, went Chet Bosworth, pushing into the room and shoving a microphone in Wulf's face.

"Warlord Wulf. What just happened here? I think you owe Willow and Genevieve an explanation, not to mention the whole world watching. What do you have to say for yourself? Explain this behavior to your adoring fans."

Adoring fans? I nearly choked on that one but then

realized one of those adoring fans watching from home had been me—up until today. Now I was, what?

"Mate. Mine." The beast was still glowering at the camera, but the intelligence had returned to Wulf's gaze. He wasn't out of control, not anymore.

"We don't understand, Warlord. For weeks now you have been getting to know Willow, Genevieve and the other candidates. Is there something wrong with the two finalists? Something you're not sharing?" Jeez, Chet was digging for dirt now.

Soon that attention-obsessed narcissist would turn his laser sights to me.

No. No way I was talking on camera with Atlan cum coating the insides of my thighs.

Wulf stared down at Chet as if the man were an insect. "Willow. No. Genevieve. No."

I glanced up as one of the cameramen in the hallway swung toward me, no doubt zooming in on my flushed cheeks, swollen lips and guilty expression. Yes, that had been me, fucking against the door, coming all over Wulf's big, hard, alien cock.

I'd certainly helped the ratings, but I'd ruined the show. They could fire me, but I had no doubt Tanner and Emma were watching with Lucy from home, on live television. I was not going to talk about alien sex on live TV. Nope. Not doing it. The interrogation Chet no doubt was salivating over was not going to happen.

It was time to get the hell out of here before I broke down as Wulf's gaze shifted my way. He kept staring, his focus too intense to ignore. Wulf had a life on The Colony. I had two little kids who needed my love and affection. I couldn't go to space. That had been settled for me when I'd learned kids couldn't go. Something about not being legally eligible to make a life-altering decision for themselves until they came of age. Whatever. I'd moved on. Wulf would, too.

We were doomed to only a quickie. Two orgasms were all I was going to get. We weren't going to have recorded dates. Walks in the park holding hands. I couldn't. I had to deal with Jimmy Steel, and being in front of a camera made it pretty hard for me to remain anonymous, especially with Jimmy. I obeyed or he hurt me. That had been a chance I was willing to take. I'd told him no a dozen times. But then he'd threatened the kids, and they *weren't* a risk of any kind.

If the last thirty minutes hadn't made it obvious enough, Wulf was honorable. He'd been courteous with the finalists, even though his beast hadn't been interested. While he might have kidnapped me to a back room to ravish me, he'd asked for consent. More than once. He hadn't fucked me because I was an available *hole* for his cock. He'd said on repeat that I was his. His mate.

Mine.

Even if my life turned into fantasyland, once he found out I was breaking the law—even if I was doing so against my will—he'd break it off. I was practically a drug dealer, and there was nothing honorable about that. He deserved better. He really did. He deserved the gorgeous, educated supermodel. He deserved the fantasy life.

There was nothing fantasy-like about my existence. Not anymore. Wulf would find out the truth, and he would break it off and break my heart. Lingering now would only make it worse.

Being short helped as I ducked beneath the arm of a cameraman and fled. People followed, but I pushed through the crowd and then, thankfully, got lost in the sea of audience members who were leaving the building. I heard a roar and knew Wulf had discovered me missing. Keeping my chin down, I made it to my car.

Wulf was somewhere inside losing his shit. He'd done it once, and they'd caught it on camera. No doubt they were doing it again. I had to assume they were ready this time and must've pulled in some of the testing center guards—huge Atlans like Wulf—to try and restrain him. I could only imagine the ratings. The show must go on. So would my life here on Earth.

Alone.

4

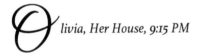

livia, Her House, 9:15 PM

LUCY MUST HAVE HEARD my car pull up in the driveway because when I rushed through the front door, she was standing right there.

I froze. "Hey."

"Don't hey me." She tossed her arms up in the air. "What the hell, woman?"

I blushed and couldn't look her in the eyes. "I had no idea that was going to happen."

"Obviously," she said, her voice laced heavily with sarcasm.

Lucy liked to pull herself together for work, in a cute outfit and full makeup, but tonight her red hair was up in a sloppy bun and she didn't even have lip gloss on.

The house was quiet, so I assumed the kids were asleep. It was nine fifteen, way past their bedtime. I had no doubt she'd tried to get them down promptly so she could watch the show without being climbed on or asked for juice.

"Are you going to let me past the front door?"

She uncrossed her arms and stepped back, although she followed right on my heels into the living room. The house was small, so it wasn't as if she was going to lose me. I dropped down onto my couch that was more comfort than cute, and inwardly winced. My pussy was sore. I hadn't had sex in... God, over two years, and it hadn't been with an Atlan beast. Looking back, my old boyfriend had a pencil dick in comparison to what I'd just gotten off on.

In the moment I'd been too turned on to consider how big Wulf was. Now I felt like I'd been pummeled on the inside. I bit my lip, trying not to grin. Pummeled? More like pounded.

Too bad I couldn't do it again.

"Start talking," Lucy ordered.

"Was it as crazy on TV as it was live?" I wondered. I mentally crossed my fingers that they'd stopped recording.

Lucy dropped onto the couch, turned so her knee was bent and she faced me. The light caught on the little ring in her nose. She took my hand and gave me a green-with-envy look. "Sweetie, he knocked down the set to get to you. He toppled a camera and crushed that twat's microphone." She leaned back, making a fist. "God, that was awesome. Then, when he carried you away..." Her voice turned wistful, and she stared at me intently. "You're going to tell me every single thing that happened when he closed the door to that back room. Every. Single. Thing."

"They didn't switch to a commercial?" I asked, holding out hope it wasn't as bad as I thought.

She laughed. "They *skipped* commercials."

I put a hand over my face. "Oh my God."

"Spill."

I bit my lip. "He thinks I'm his mate."

"Duh," she said as if she were still in middle school. "Everyone on Earth knows that."

I dropped my hand and stared at her wide-eyed. "On *Earth?*"

"It was live and broadcast around the world. You know they have testing centers all over, and he's going to do a tour with his mate once the show is over." When I didn't respond, she continued, "I'm going to take your favorite eye shadow set as my own if you don't stop stalling."

I gasped, knowing how much she loved the colors in my palette. "We... we, um... he... God." I knew my face was as red as her hair.

"You had sex with him?" she squeaked. "Please tell me you had sex with him."

I nodded. She could imagine what she wanted, but I wasn't telling her about how he'd propped me up on the chair and ate me out. There seemed to be no secrets between me and Wulf... and the entire world, but I'd keep that hot bit of fun to myself.

"Beasts mate standing up," she said as if reading from a textbook.

"They do," I verified. "Against the door so that no one could get in."

She sighed and rolled her eyes as if she were eating a delectable cream puff. "Against the door? That is so fucking hot."

"It was." My inner walls clenched as if remembering, too.

"No wonder they couldn't get in." Lucy wrapped her arms around her middle and laughed with glee. "They were trying to break down the door. Couldn't you hear them pounding?"

"Um, I was distracted."

"By something else pounding?" She waggled her eyebrows like a clown, and it was my turn to laugh.

"Something like that." I put my hand over my eyes. We were not having this discussion. This was a weird mushroom trip, a dream. Someone had slipped something into my water bottle at work.

"Details. How big? How hard? What did he say? Did he smell good? Was he gentle? Was it him or the beast? How big?"

I arched a brow. "You already asked that."

"Well... how big?"

"Beast big."

Her mouth fell open as if imagining, but when I didn't offer up more information, she started using her hands as visual aids.

I answered her questions, one by one until she was satisfied, but left out the special stuff. Because while it had been hot as hell and totally wild, it *had* been special. At least to me.

"Now what?" she finally asked me.

"Now?" I grabbed one of Emma's stuffed animals off the back of the couch and hugged it. "Now I sit here with you and chat. Then I get a shower..." I looked at the clock on the kitchen wall and popped up from the couch. "Shit, I have to hurry. You sure you don't mind staying a little longer. I'll only be gone about an hour."

"Delivering meals to the elderly?"

I bit my lip. Lying to my BFF sucked, but I had no choice. She was my only babysitter, and I'd needed her to watch the kids on the previous drops. I wasn't getting her involved in my mess. Sure, I'd tell her I had sex with an Atlan beast behind a closed door on live TV, but I couldn't endanger her life by knowing the truth about my drug runs for Jimmy Steel. The less she knew, the better.

I was a terrible liar. At the beginning, when Jimmy had first confronted me a week after Greg's death, I'd been expected to do his dirty work during the day and my story had been plausible. Now, late at night, not so much.

I only nodded and turned toward the bathroom.

"You can tell me, you know." Lucy wasn't dumb, and I was sure she had some idea about what I was up to, or at least that it wasn't good.

I faced her. Shook my head. "Thanks for being here," I said, wishing I could tell her the truth.

Plausible deniability was on her side. Besides, if I got caught and went to jail, I needed Lucy to watch the kids. I had no one else.

"What are you going to do about Wulf?" she asked, thankfully changing the subject. Although Wulf wasn't something I wanted to talk about either.

"Nothing," I said, feeling silly standing there. I had to hurry, I had to answer her questions first. I grabbed a plastic dinosaur off the floor and put it in the toy box in the corner. "I sneaked out."

"Yeah, it was on TV. Wulf lost his shit. Again. They shot him with tranquilizer darts like he was an elephant or something."

My eyes widened. "Shit. They did not." I'd heard him bellow, stuff crashing. But no. Just no.

"Oh, they did. Took three to take him down. They had to cut the broadcast with a pile of alien hotties piling on top of him and that living mannequin, Chet Bosworth, promising to keep everyone updated in the next episode."

I frowned and turned to face her. "That was the finale. There is no *next episode*."

She shrugged. "Sweetie, you started it all back up again. Now it's all about the Beauty and the Beast."

"You've got to be kidding," I said, grabbing a few little cars and putting them away. "Beauty? Me? You've seen Genevieve and Willow."

She stood and went around the coffee table, grabbing her sweatshirt. "You always do this, talk yourself down. You're wonderful and it's clear a hot Atlan sees it, even if you can't see it for yourself."

I glanced down at myself.

"Not all guys like to fuck a twig," she snapped. "Meat on your bones is healthy."

As if what I had was meat. I had meat and potatoes and an apple pie. Right on my hips and ass.

"It's not going to happen," I said with a sigh. "I have Tanner and Emma. You know I tried to get tested, but I have dependents. I can't leave them on Earth. Before you say it, I can't take them with me. It's not allowed. They aren't old enough to decide for themselves, so they have to stay unless I already have a mate."

"That's a stupid rule," she muttered.

I only shrugged because I didn't make the rules. It would have been great though, to get away from Jimmy Steel. Tonight was it, the last drug run; then Greg's debt was paid off. I could then start saving for the kids' college funds. Hell, for groceries. Moving out of town was one thing, but moving to a different planet would definitely get the jerk off my back. This was the end of it. One of Jimmy's goons had left the package in my garage—their usual drop-off spot— sometime the night before and had left a note as to the wheres and whens of this last drop.

Soon enough, I'd be free.

"Ant Wivvy!" Tanner came running down the hall and hugged me as if he were a monkey climbing a tree. At four he was independent, but he still liked to hug and love on me. I knew it wouldn't last, so I loved every single snuggle. Leaning down, I wrapped my arms around his little body, currently covered by cute dinosaur pj's. He looked so much like his father that it made my heart hurt.

"I thought you were asleep, peanut."

"I'm thirsty."

"Of course, you are," I replied, kissing the top of his head. "Where's your sister? Is she asleep?"

"Yep. She's just a baby." Which was true. Emma wasn't even two yet, and she slept like a log. Tanner, on the other hand, would wake to the sound of bare feet on carpet. I wondered if that was natural for him, or if it was because he'd always been listening, waiting for his dad to come home late at night. I'd never know, and neither of his parents were ever coming home again.

I squeezed him a little too tight, and he wiggled free in protest.

"He's going to show up, you know," Lucy said, her voice soft.

My head whipped in her direction.

"What?" She didn't know about Jimmy Steel, and her words freaked me out.

"Wulf. When he wakes up, he'll be at the door."

My heart slowed, then picked right back up again at the idea of Wulf showing up here, at our little house. Angry? Hurt? I didn't know.

"A woof's coming here?" Tanner asked, looking excited about the idea.

"He will not," I told both of them.

53

She gave me a fierce hug. "He will. You're his mate and you ran off. He's going to find you. Come on, squirt, let's get you back to bed."

"Yay! We're getting a woof!" Tanner cheered, running down the hall to his bedroom, clearly forgetting he'd wanted a drink. It seemed he wanted a pet Atlan more.

She followed him down the hall while I went to take my speed shower. Locking the door, I leaned against it. I thought of a different door I'd leaned against just a little while ago. The dainty lock might keep Tanner and Emma out, but it wasn't going to do anything to keep Wulf away. The lock I'd firmly placed around my heart? I worried he may have already blown that open.

Maybe I did, too.

5

ulf, Interstellar Brides Center, Holding Cell

WHAT WAS WRONG WITH ME? Was I injured? I'd never felt this... heavy except when the Hive—

No. I was not going to think about that. Not with the taste of my mate's pussy on my lips.

My mate.

Blinking my eyes open, I tried to sit, realized that my body was too big to be waking from sleep. Then why had I been unconscious? Fuck, I was not myself. I was not in control.

My beast had not retreated. I was in beast mode.

Rising slowly, I swung my giant legs over the side of the laughably small bed, and my beast growled as the room began to spin and nausea made bile rise into my throat. What had happened to me?

A female stood inside the room, blocking a door so small that I would need to crouch to walk through. She cleared her throat. No, not my mate. Not Olivia Mercier. I'd know her sound anywhere. Her scent. Her touch. Her *taste*. I struggled to hold back the mating fever that clawed its way through me as I recognized this woman was not my mate. She was not mine, so why was she here?

She was either incredibly brave or a complete idiot.

"Are you going to be reasonable, Warlord, or do I need to call in the guards to shoot you in the ass with more tranquilizer before they carry you to the transport pad."

Her voice was gentle but laced with steel. I was on her turf now, wherever the fuck I was.

"Mate," my beast responded. "Where?"

"Not here. She went home, Wulf." She was not a threat. She was small. Female. Human. Like our mate. The soft, sweet-tasting female I'd fucked. Her smell clung to my body, haunting me, which was probably a good thing.

"Where?"

The warden made a scolding sound. "They hit you with enough tranquilizer to keep an elephant down for twelve hours."

"Not elephant."

That made her laugh, and I welcomed the sound, made sure my beast focused on the female and her amusement. This was not battle. We were not in danger. Despite that, I was very close to losing control of him, but knowing my cock was covered in Olivia's scent, that I had her taste in my mouth eased me enough to hold on. I needed my mating cuffs from the glass box on the stage. They were mine. No, one set was mine, but the other belonged to Olivia Mercier and I would see her wear them, devote myself to her care until my last breath.

"I have to give you Atlans credit," Warden Egara said, still smiling. I'd met her when I'd first arrived on the planet.

"You do have a one-track mind when it comes to your females." She stepped farther into the room, and into the light when she realized I was not going to go into a killing frenzy.

Warden Egara was familiar to me, a female who worked at the Earth's Interstellar Brides Processing Center where I'd spent most of the past three weeks. Her dark hair was pulled back into a tight bun, she wore the ridiculous shoes the females referred to as *high heels* and her uniform had the Coalition Fleet insignia for the Brides Program on her chest. She was intelligent and responsible for the happiness of many warriors and fighters in the Coalition because she was in charge of the female volunteers from Earth. She'd coordinated often with Rachel about finding mates for The Colony.

She was an ally. A friend. She would know where my female was and how I could find her. Egara lived on this planet and, since she was also human, would know the ways and customs to help me find my mate.

She had to help me before the beast decided to go on a scent-driven rampage and hunt the streets for the one female I knew was in this city. If my beast went hunting, I'd kill a lot of humans before I found her, and he *would* find her. But once I did, they'd have to put me to death because I would not be able to regain control. I'd be lost. I was that far gone, especially now that I knew she was out there, separate from me.

I was alone. I should not be alone. I'd found my mate. We should not be apart.

"Mate," I said again as if I suddenly had a one-word vocabulary. I knew plenty of words, even in the Earth English we were using, but that one word summed up everything I cared about at the moment. Her. Olivia Mercier. "Mine."

Warden Egara crossed her arms in a way I recognized as irritation from the few human females I knew on The Colony. She even tilted her head and raised one eyebrow as Rachel did when she was about to scold one of them. Or me, earlier on the comm call.

"Listen, Wulf, you really made a mess of things," she continued.

"Mate."

One hand went up. "Stop. I know you want to know where Olivia is—"

Olivia. Her name was beautiful. Soft, like her breasts. Her stomach. Her round ass when I'd cupped the fullness of her in my hands. When I found her I would—

"Hey." She waved that hand in circles in front of me. "Earth to Wulf. Stay with me. You need to focus." Warden Egara stepped even closer, within reach, and snapped her tiny fingers in front of my face with a distinct, clipped noise that got the beast's attention. "Focus, Wulf. You want your mate? Don't you? You want me to help you find her? Convince her to accept you and your mating cuffs? Yes? That's what you want?"

"Yes. Mine." I scowled. She spoke to me as if I were a child. I was not. For a moment I considered standing, towering over her, backing her down a bit, but she was female. Small. No threat. That would be dishonorable, and as an ally I didn't want to anger her. Such an act would not get me any closer to the female I wanted. Olivia.

"Listen," she said, her voice a little louder. "Are you listening to me?"

"Yes, Warden Egara." I fought hard, forcing my beast into submission, reasoning with him that it was the only way we were both going to get what we wanted. Out of this cell. Past the guards without killing one of them. To be honest, he didn't care much about the killing, not if it meant gaining access to our female. Our mate. I took a deep breath, another. Unclenched my fists with substantial effort. When I cleared my throat, I was myself again. Barely. My body had shrunk back to... normal. The Earth outfit they'd forced me to wear fit my body once more, but the fabric was in tatters.

She offered me a small smile. "Thank God. You're back."

I looked up into gray eyes filled with sympathy, but no pity and no compromise. Warden Egara was a commander in her own way. "I'm on your side, but I have to advise you, do not let him out again unless you have the mating cuffs on and Olivia is yours. Do you hear me? You've already caused a huge public relations nightmare with that stunt you pulled earlier."

"It wasn't a stunt," I countered. "She's my mate. The beast recognized her. I had no control."

She studied me. "You're too close to the edge, Warlord. The governor should have sent someone else."

I nodded. "Agreed. I was prepared to transport to Atlan for execution. I did not want to be here."

"Coming to Earth and being on a reality TV show is not an acceptable alternative."

"I hope you do not think the choice was mine."

She sighed. "Rachel. Still an optimist after everything she's been through."

"Yes." The warden spoke true. Governor Maxim's mate refused to surrender hope for any male on The Colony. We all loved her for it. We fought harder, hung on longer, for her. Hoping she was right. Hoping a mate like her would save us as she had saved Maxim and Ryston.

The warden's small hand came to rest on my shoulder,

but I did not look her in the eye. I did not want to see pity now, where before there had been none. Death was a fact of life for a warrior. Accepted as inevitable, especially for those like me who'd been captured by the Hive. I'd survived their torture. I had managed to escape, and yet, in the end, it would be my own inner beast who would kill me. Now or later made little difference to a beast with no female. There were only two things we focused on once the mating fever took us over: battle and fucking.

I'd fucked Olivia Mercier, but she was not here with me. No cuffs were on our wrists. There was no other living creature that my beast would answer to, not now. Not me. No Atlan commander or warlord would dare issue an order to a beast in mating fever. My beast would rage against and defy even Prime Nial himself. The beast answered to no one and nothing but the small female who consumed every thought, every sense.

I was hers. Olivia literally held my life in her hands. If she needed me to die, I would die. It was that simple and that complex. What she needed, I would provide. No matter the cost.

"Death means nothing, Warden," I explained.

"It does to me." She squeezed my shoulder, the tiny amount of pressure surprisingly calming. "And to the people you leave behind. Olivia Mercier is your mate. I am pleased you have found her. So be it. We can still save the show, and the others' chances of getting a mate. We can save you, too."

I looked up into her face now. "How?"

She smiled. "Well, you are going to go to Olivia's house. I will give you the address."

My beast settled, content. He was going to get what he

wanted. Egara was going to tell us exactly where to find our female.

She held up her hand, the first finger pointing straight up in the air. "You, Warlord Wulf, are going to act like a gentleman, not a beast. You are going to court her properly, not go all wild and feral on her like you already did. Do you hear me? You will have two days of privacy to convince her to be yours. That's all the time I can give you."

I frowned. Two days? "I don't understand."

She grinned, and the look was another I recognized on human females, this time from Kristen. Smug. Mischievous. Dangerous. I did not envy Kristen's mates, Tyrnan and Hunt, when their warrior mate made a face similar to what Egara had now. "I hid her employee file. She was part-time, hired solely for the series, and no one pays any attention to makeup staff on set. I contacted her boss, a woman named Lucy Vandermark. She is refusing to give out Olivia's personal information to the media. Even though her face is plastered from here to Siberia on every form of social media, no one knows who she is. I spoke to this woman, and we agreed to buy you some time."

I did not know this Lucy, but I was thankful to her. "Time for what? I will claim her, offer her my mating cuffs, take her home to The Colony."

"It's not that simple," she replied stepping back to pace the small room. "Despite your... scene, the producer has demanded you continue the program as planned. You are under a contractual obligation to make a trip to New York to be interviewed, with your new bride, on late-night television. You were supposed to place your mating cuffs on one of the others tonight, on live television. Seeing you on one knee, basically proposing, was the crown jewel of promotion for the series.

They are talking about doing another show, with another male from The Colony. But they need to give the public what they want, and that's you, on your knees, asking Olivia to be yours in front of the entire world. That's you and your new mate making goo-goo eyes at each other on international television."

I must have looked as confused as I felt because the warden raised her hand and swiped it through the air as if swatting at an insect. "There are already memes out there. Some of them are actually very entertaining."

"What is a meme? And what the fuck are *goo-goo eyes* and how do I make them? My eyes will not change, Warden. They have been contaminated with Hive—"

"Never mind. It's another live broadcast, but this time on a talk show. This will ensure that the Brides Program is seen in a positive light, that the whole world sees you and Olivia have your happily ever after and convince every other woman on Earth that they can have the same if they volunteer. You and your new bride have to go, sit in chairs and answer questions. They want the entire world to witness the two of you together and make sure everyone watching sees exactly how devoted and loving you are to your new bride."

That made my chest puff out. Devoted? Loving? I would love her until she screamed like she had earlier. She would be satisfied. Adored. Worshipped. Protected. The beast rose and spoke before I could stop him. "Mine."

"Stop that." The warden scolded me like I was a small boy, and my beast retreated with a grumble but didn't argue. He was listening. I did not care about this television interview as long as I was with Olivia and my mating cuffs were around her wrists.

"I have two days. Then what? How do we do this talking show? I still do not understand how to make a goo-goo eye.

Will Olivia understand what is required?" I wanted all the intel on this situation, not just a little bit. I didn't want surprises, and if she didn't want my beast to take over, Warden Egara would make sure there were none.

Warden Egara chuckled. "Yes. Olivia will know exactly what I am talking about."

Good. I settled more at that information. I would not embarrass myself asking the warden again, not when my mate could provide the information about these strange eyes.

Egara continued. "You have two days with her. Private days. Then you and Olivia get on a plane to New York."

"A human airplane?" I asked. I'd seen images of them, and I was appalled.

She nodded her head. "Yes."

"No." Flying metal death traps. Primitive. Running on fossilized fuels and combustion. Barbaric. It would be safer to walk.

"Yes. It's perfectly safe, and we are trying to make you appear normal."

"I am normal," I countered.

That made her laugh. "Not on Earth, you're not, sweetheart. Not even close."

I let that one go. She was an ally, and I was wasting time arguing with her about inconsequential things. "Two days. Then television. Then home?"

"Not exactly." She cleared her throat and glanced away for a moment. "You messed this up, Wulf. I'm not going to lie. The reason Lindsey and I came up with this idea was to showcase how honorable, strong and devoted you Coalition guys are as mates. We wanted to entice human women not just to volunteer to be a bride, but to *request* The Colony specifically."

"The brides can request a planet?"

"Yes. Most don't, but yes, they can. Since fighters from almost every world are on The Colony, we pushed that element during all the promotions for the show. While you might have been the star of the program, you may have missed these details. We made sure everyone knows about the veterans there, that they are strong, that they survived capture by the enemies and that many of them are now outcasts on their home worlds, including some human males who have fought in the Hive wars and not been allowed to return to Earth."

"That makes us sound like pathetic fools."

She shook her head. "No. Trust me. It makes you relatable. Likable. Wounded in a way that a lot of human women, for whatever reason, seem to have an instinctive need to heal." Now her hands were on her hips. "Being a veteran makes you more desirable, not less. But you were supposed to choose between the two finalists, Genevieve and Willow. Instead you embarrassed them, knocked down a cameraman, crushed poor Chet's microphone and scared him so badly he needed to change his boxers—"

She chuckled, but I had no idea what a boxer was, so I waited. I had not seen any boxes on him during the show.

"And then you carried an unknown female off camera, fucked her up against a door on live television, then turned into an out-of-control monster threatening to kill everyone in the building when she tried to walk away. You were tranqed on live TV and fell like a redwood." She shook her head at me. "Not the image of an honorable, dependable warrior we were going for."

Hearing her say it like that... She was correct. My actions may have cost many contaminated warriors on The Colony their chance at a bride. I could not live with that. "I apologize that my actions caused that result. Tell me what I must do to make this right. But know this, Olivia Mercier is mine. I will not leave without her."

"I know that and you know that, but Olivia doesn't know that. The President of the United States doesn't know that. Congress doesn't know that. The public at large doesn't know that."

"I do not care about any of those other humans."

"Well, you have to, because Olivia did *not* volunteer to be an Interstellar Bride. She did not sign a waiver for the program as a participant in the *Bachelor Beast* television show. As far as all of Earth is concerned, she is a citizen of Earth and remains under our protection and our laws, not Coalition laws. She has to choose you, Wulf. First, you'll have two days to convince her to appear with you on live television and convince the world that you two are madly in love."

"She is mine."

"It doesn't work like that here."

I took a breath to interrupt, but she held up one finger and I waited.

"Two days until the talk show in New York. After that, she must be willing to leave the planet with you. Willing. After New York—and depending on how things go at her house—you will have seven days left until you have to get the hell off this planet and go back to The Colony. Do you hear me? Seven days, and that includes your time in New York."

"That is not enough time."

"Tough luck. This is Earth law, not Coalition. Your permission to be on this planet expires in exactly nine days." She checked a small device on her wrist and scrunched up her nose as she did some kind of mental calculation. "Yes.

Nine days, three hours and twenty-seven minutes until I have to transport you off this rock."

"She is mine. She will come with me."

"Let's hope you are right, Wulf. But I want to make it clear, she is not a volunteer. You have to convince her to leave behind everything she's ever known to go with you. I can't transport her unless she is wearing your mating cuffs."

"I should have thirty days to woo a bride. That is in the bride contracts."

Shaking her head, she clarified, "Listen to me. She. Is. Not. A. Bride. She did *not* sign a contract. Get that into your head. She's a regular old citizen who has not even contemplated leaving her life on Earth behind. *Your* permission to be here expires in just over nine days. You *had* thirty days on Earth to select a bride. You've already spent three weeks, twenty-one of your thirty days, here on the show. The fact that you did not choose one of the contestants is a technicality the government here does not care about. You have nine days left, and then, bride or no bride, you will be transported off this planet."

"Fuck."

"Now you are beginning to understand."

"How do I make a human female choose me?"

She offered me a small smile. "Every woman is different, Wulf."

"That is not helpful."

She sighed. "Be honest. Be yourself. You are a worthy, honorable male. She will see that. I've given you a two-day head start. That's all I can do. After that, the paparazzi will find you and you'll be living in a fishbowl. It'll be a media circus."

"What is paparazzi?"

"They follow famous people around for money. Invade

their privacy. Take lots of pictures. Write stories about them, like Lindsey does on The Colony, but not as nice. The more shocking and scandalous, the more money they make. Some famous people want the attention. Some don't. It's complicated."

"No. I need no attention. They will not follow my female." I did not like the sound of that. I knew Hunter Kiel's mate, the human female Lindsey. She told stories about the warriors on The Colony. Made us feel valued. Seen. Not forgotten. This sounded completely different. "If they go near my mate, I will crush them."

"Only if you want to go to human prison."

"My beast would not submit to human authorities."

"Exactly. So let's keep the crushing of asshole humans to a minimum, shall we?"

My beast growled, but this time the warden wasn't laughing.

"I'll take you to the men's locker room where you can shower."

"I do not wish to lose my mate's scent," I countered quickly.

She eyed me. "Trust me, Warlord. Scent or not, you need to shower. Your female will want you to be clean and you're... not. After, I'll take you to Olivia."

"I will have my cuffs on her," I vowed.

A heavy sigh escaped her lips. "About that. The show has your cuffs."

I stood and bellowed, "What?"

"You destroyed a set, ruined two weeks of planned programming. Don't get me wrong, they're thrilled for this twist, but they won't risk you getting those cuffs on your mate off-screen."

"They are mine. They have no right."

"The cuffs are on their way to New York waiting for the tell-all program. There, you will put them on your mate on live TV."

The idea was horrible, holding my cuffs hostage for something they called ratings. I had no choice. I had to go to New York in order to end the show in a favorable light for my fellow fighters. I also had to get my fucking cuffs and get them on Olivia Mercier. My focus was absolute.

"I am not pleased," I said.

"Yes, I figured it wouldn't make you happy." She waved me over with her hand. "Come on. Shower, then your mate."

I looked down at myself. The tattered clothes. I had streaks of dirt on my hands and the clothing as if I'd been dragged across a dirty floor. I probably had. If I were to see my mate again, I needed to make a good impression. Anything was better than the first, except being filthy.

6

 *ulf*

Warden Egara personally drove me in a small metal and plastic vehicle to Olivia Mercier's residence. It hadn't been as simple as it sounded, for I was at least a foot taller than almost all humans, even more than that for a large section of the population. Therefore I was very noticeable. Since I'd made such a mess of the live broadcast, I was as famous as ever. This was why I was grateful for the dark of night, which offered us some hint of anonymity.

I didn't like the concept of being well-known. Of these... paparazzi following my female because of it. In fact it made me practically itch with the idea that I and my mate were everyone's focus. Their favorite topic of speculation. From what Warden Egara had said, I was the center of all of Earth's rabid attention.

That made it very difficult to be able to leave the testing center without being followed. I was recognizable. If

Warden Egara was to give me two days to keep the producers and others away, I needed to remain hidden. Since anonymity was not an option, I had to disappear.

At first the warden was going to drive me in her own vehicle, hidden, but I was too big to lie down in the back seat as she drove past the front gates, past the hordes of people I'd been told were there hoping to get a glimpse of me through the walls. They hadn't left since the show began. Day or night, they waited, some in tents. I found it all very unsettling.

Warden Egara had found something called a van, which was much larger than her tiny human mover, and the larger vehicle had no windows in the back. I was able to hide there while she drove fifteen minutes to Olivia's home. I'd seen some of the planet during the program's scheduled activities for me and the females, the dates I'd endured, and had not been very intrigued. All that interested me now was seeing Olivia, not the place called Florida. It smelled of swamp and rot and water. Too much water.

It reminded me that the Hive preferred places with water for their integration centers. That thought brought my beast roaring in rage, and a growl escaped my throat before I could wrest control from him.

"Calm down back there," Warden Egara said from her seat. "I'm pulling into the driveway."

Olivia. I needed her. Badly. Now. Right fucking now.

Not to fuck, but to keep me sane.

"My apologies, Warden Egara," I murmured. I appreciated the woman's efforts to assist me. I knew she was going above and beyond her duties, and certainly outside what the program's organizers would wish.

"Accepted. I know you're on the edge, Wulf, and I'm taking a huge risk setting you loose like this. If I had any sense, I would have had the guards stun you again and drag you to transport."

"Why didn't you?" I was serious. She was correct. That would have been the more prudent choice.

She pulled the van to a stop and sat in silence for a full minute before speaking again. I used the time to regain my normal size, shove the beast back into his place inside me.

"Because you deserve better, Warlord. You sacrificed enough. You suffered enough. You deserve to be happy."

With that, she opened her door and hopped out to walk around to the back. When the door opened, I waited until she motioned for me to climb out. Which I did, rather stiffly.

"I feel like a parent, like I'm dropping you off for the prom."

The more time I spent on Earth, the more I realized I did not know about these humans and their rituals. "What is the prom?"

"Just a fancy dance where all the teenagers dress up in really fancy clothes and flirt and dance and—" She stopped mid-sentence and shook her head. "Never mind. It's kind of a rite of passage. It's courting. Wooing. It's part of growing up."

"I shall not become any taller than I already am. This prom will not work on me."

"I know. It's a lot more about looking good to try to get the girl—or the boy—you're interested in, to be interested in you."

Understanding dawned. "It is a mating ritual?"

"Yes. I suppose it is." She pointed to the small house. "That's Olivia's place."

I really wished I had my mating cuffs, felt vulnerable without them. "Thank you."

"Good luck. It's late, Wulf. Almost midnight. She's

probably asleep. So don't pound down her door. Knock gently. Don't scare the life out of her. Remember, be a gentleman. Woo her."

Gentleman. Wooing. Courting. Nodding, I said, "I will not fail."

"Good. Go get her." Warden Egara climbed back into the van while I walked to inspect the door she had pointed to. The living quarters were small boxes with squares cut in the walls and a rectangular entrance. Similar small boxes lined the street on both sides as far as I could see. Foliage adorned the landscape, lush and tropical, similar to perhaps Viken. The dwellings looked nearly identical except for the golden numbers attached to the front.

Once I stood before the door, painted black, staring at the numbers 432, Warden Egara waved, wished me luck on my first date and took off like she was being chased.

I didn't know what she meant, as I had been forced to endure many of the human dates for the television show, but I was nervous. My palms were damp, and I wiped them on my pants. I was alone now. The sound of small wild animals filled the night air, but otherwise it was silent.

I had nowhere else to go if Olivia did not allow me to enter her home. The warden had been right when she'd scolded me earlier. While Olivia had consented to my mouth and cock giving her pleasure, she had not volunteered for the television program, nor had she volunteered to be a bride. She had been working, and I'd carried her off. Practically kidnapped her in front of the entire planet, on the Earthen version of a live comm broadcast.

I didn't regret the action in the least. I'd shown honesty in my desire for her. My obsession. But now I would do it properly and obtain her agreement to wear my cuffs. Her residence was small. I was glad we would not permanently reside here. I was too large. It was too hot. There was too much water. She would be content with the quarters on The Colony, much more spacious... and arid.

I would not have to endure a swamp. Pollution. Water and mold and the clinging liquid that hovered in the air like an invisible coat.

I knocked on the door. Hard.

Two days. I had two days until Warden Egara returned.

I took a breath. Waited.

Screams came from inside. The door finally opened. I expected to face Olivia, but the female before me was not my mate.

I frowned down at the woman with red hair and a ring in her nose as if she were from Trion.

"You are not Olivia Mercier."

Her mouth fell open as she looked up, up, up at me. "You're Warlord Wulf. Oh my God."

More screams made my heart lurch and my beast snarl. I gently moved the woman out of the way, ducked my head and entered the home, afraid someone was harming my mate.

I froze once inside the entrance. Two small humans were running around a couch waving their arms. They were emitting the screams, which made me cringe. At the sight of me, they stopped in their tracks and stared.

I stared back.

The older one was a boy, the younger, a girl. Both had blond hair and chubby cheeks and were clearly related. They wore what humans called pajamas, the boy having an odd spiked animal image on the front. The girl had small flowers all over hers. Around their necks were tied cloths that dangled down their backs. For what, I had no idea. I guessed, if humans aged comparably to Atlans, they were around two and four years old.

"You're big," the boy said.

He wasn't scared of me, more wary, and that was surprising. I scared full-grown human adults, and yet this small child was only curious.

"My mother made me eat lots of nutritional food when I was your age."

He puckered his little brow. "Like brock-wi?"

"Is it nutritional?" I asked.

The boy cocked his head. "Woocy, is brock-wi nutrinaw?" he asked, trying his best to sound out the large word.

"Yes."

His eyes widened, and he looked me over from head to toe. After my shower, Warden Egara had provided me with new clothing, pants and a shirt that, while sized for an Atlan, were styled more like human attire.

"If I eat it, can I grow to be as big as him?" He pointed at me as he asked the woman.

"It's possible," she said.

"I want brock-wi for my bedtime snack! I want to be huge!" he shouted, then ran in circles around my legs. The little girl, who'd remained silent this entire time, watched her brother. Seeing that he wasn't fazed or afraid, she followed him in behavior.

I looked to the woman called Woocy as the children ran around and around my legs. "Where is Olivia Mercier?" I asked.

"She had something to do but will be back soon," she replied. That was not a sufficient explanation.

"Something to do? It is late. What could she be doing that cannot wait? It is not safe for my female to be out at night. She should be home. Safe. With her mate protecting her."

She raised an eyebrow and crossed her arms. There was that gods-be-damned pose from a human female again. "Yes, it's late," she confirmed. "Yet here you are. A stranger banging on the door. Was it safe to let you in?"

I stared at her, my beast appalled. "I would never hurt a female. Or a child."

The children began to slow, and I imagined they might topple over soon from dizziness.

"It's still late, Warlord. I don't know you."

"You do," I countered. "You said my name."

Her mouth snapped shut with the click of her teeth.

"I will wait."

"Of course." A smile spread across her face. "You should sit so I don't get a crook in my neck."

She was a small human, like Olivia, but slender like a male human. She had no blatant curves, no lushness to her physique like my mate had. My beast was not interested in this female, thinking that she would be bony, not soft to fuck like Olivia.

I looked between the seating choices and selected the couch, the largest and most likely not to break beneath my weight.

"Let Wulf sit down," Woocy said, and the kids stopped as if stunned with an ion pistol.

I took that advantage and went to the couch and settled upon it. I had to push the small table in front of it farther away so my legs could fit.

"You're the woof?" the boy asked.

"That is my name," I replied.

"I'm Tanner. I'm a superhero." He tugged at the fabric that draped down his back.

I looked to Woocy.

"He's wearing a cape," she said, although that didn't explain anything.

"Me, too! Emma!" the little girl said, patting her chest.

These two reminded me of the new little ones running around The Colony.

"Hello, Tanner and Emma," I replied, then looked to Woocy. "You have... nice children."

She laughed. "They're not mine. They're Olivia's."

My gaze dropped back to the children. My mate had children? That meant... "She said she was not mated."

Lucy shook her head, her red curls bouncing. She settled into the chair beside the couch. "She's not... mated. They are her niece and nephew. Their p.a.r.e.n.t.s.d.i.e.d." She spelled the last two words.

It took me a moment to process what she'd said, especially in a different language, but I finally understood the reason why she didn't say the word straightaway.

"That is s.a.d," I replied.

"Can I sit wif you, Woof?" Tanner asked, coming to stand beside my right leg. Emma remained closer to Woocy as if still unsure of me.

"Yes," I replied. I was used to The Colony children climbing on me, but most of them had been born and raised among huge warriors and were accustomed to us. Wyatt, the Hunter Kiel's son, had come to The Colony older but had quickly become fearless like his father. I had to assume I was the first warrior these children had ever seen, and it was surprising—and heartwarming—that he wasn't fearful.

I wasn't sure if I should be pleased or concerned for the trusting nature of these children with strangers.

Tanner climbed up my bent leg and sat on my thigh. On my lap. Not beside me as I'd expected. I hooked an arm around him so he didn't fall off and hit his head on the table. Children were fragile and needed protecting, no matter their planet of origin.

"So, Wulf," Woocy began.

"Woocy," I replied.

She laughed, head thrown back. "My name is Lucy." She tipped her head toward Tanner. "He's working on sounding some letters. *L*'s are hard for him."

I looked down at Tanner, who stared up at me with awe. "I think I like Woocy better," I told him, as if sharing a secret.

He giggled.

That had Emma moving. She came around to the other side and tried to climb up my leg but was too small. I hooked her waist and lifted her up so she sat on my other knee, tucked into my side.

"You should stay and play horsey," Lucy said.

I had absolutely no idea what that meant, so I moved on to more important things. "Olivia."

"Your mate?" Lucy asked, eyebrow arched. She didn't seem all that surprised. Then I remembered I'd heard her name before. So, this female was the Lucy that Warden Egara had spoken of. Lucy Vandermark. She was an ally. A friend. She was responsible for the extra time I would have to woo Olivia.

"You are her boss. You are protecting her privacy."

She nodded. "I am. I saw the show. I knew you'd come. Olivia deserves someone special, who will care about her. Love her."

I stiffened my spine. "I will. You know I am serious about Olivia."

"Yes, I know. That's why I'm helping," she said. "You being here means what exactly? Because Olivia is my friend.

She's sweet and kind and a big softy. So if you're only interested in more... door stuff and break her heart, I will take you out myself. Got it?"

"Take me out where?" I asked. "I do not wish to participate in a human date with you. I only want Olivia. She is mine. My mate. I would never hurt her. I will kill anyone who tries."

She studied me for a minute, and I sat patiently under her scrutiny. I sensed that her good judgment of me was crucial to my success with Olivia Mercier. "You sure about that?"

"Yes."

"Perfect." She smiled and leaned back, much more relaxed. "She's going to need your beast man. She thinks I'm stupid, but I'm not. She's in some bad business with some bad people."

I frowned and growled.

"He's got rumbles in his tummy!" Tanner said, then patted my chest.

I ignored him because this was important. I sensed that Lucy was worried. "Is that where she is now? With these bad people?"

She bit her lip. "I think so."

I would have jumped to my feet, but I was still buried in children. Very small, fragile children who belonged to Olivia. They would now belong to me. This little boy who kept patting me and the little girl who, when I looked down at her, had fallen asleep in my hold.

Her trust in me was great, and I was humbled.

My beast, however, was not happy with the information Lucy had shared. Another soft, rumbling growl left my throat, to be answered by a much louder, ferocious growl from the young one named Tanner.

He giggled; then it fell away. "The bad people killed my daddy and my mommy. I hate the bad people."

His words shocked Lucy, her mouth gaping open.

I was pleased. He was young. A young warrior. Despite these two protective females, he had stated the truth. Perhaps discovered it on his own.

"Where did you hear that, Tanner?" Lucy asked, leaning forward and setting her elbows on her knees. I could see the concern in her eyes. She cared for these young ones as if they were her own. "Where?"

He rose to stand on my thigh, and I supported him with my hand at his back as he straightened to his full height. "I heard Auntie talking on the phone. I am a big boy. I know what happened. I know."

Emma stirred and started to cry. Wail was a more apt description. I could practically feel her response to her big brother's upset. Lucy made a move to take her from my care, but this wee one was mine now, mine to protect. That started now, so I pulled her in snug to me to feel my strength and offer her reassurance.

"Emma." I used my deepest, softest voice. She turned to look at me, and I held her tear-filled gaze. "I am going to take care of you and your Auntie Olivia from now on. No one will ever hurt her or you or your brother ever again. Ever. Do you understand?"

"You're our woof now?" Tanner asked. I glanced at him, with his eyes wide, full of what I recognized as hope and apprehension. "I heard Woocy and Auntie talking about getting a woof."

I glanced to Lucy, who blushed.

"Four-year-olds have no filter," she mumbled.

Interesting. I wondered what, exactly, my mate had shared with her friend. She glanced away, and I spoke to

Tanner as I settled Emma against my chest. She was so small, so perfect. Innocent and she needed me. Tanner, too. "Yes. I am your Wulf now."

His eyes lit up, and he grinned so big his face had to hurt. "Can we keep you?"

"I think you better ask your Auntie O about that one, Tanner." Lucy stood and paced the room but didn't try to remove the children from my arms again. I wanted nothing more than to protest her words but could not. Not yet.

"I have two days to remain with Olivia, in secret, to court her."

She spun to face me. Her eyes bulged. "Court her? After what you did earlier on TV?"

I was not going to discuss fucking in front of children, so I only said, "Yes."

A slow grin spread across her face. "This is awesome."

Inwardly I sighed at her ready acceptance. "I am glad you agree."

She set her hand on her chest. "I'm your partner in Operation Olivia Gets A Mate."

I took a moment to process her words with my NPU.

I guessed it was my frown that had her continuing. "Olivia's my best friend. She deserves someone who can..." She cleared her throat. "Change things for the better."

"I will not tolerate any threat to her safety."

"Good. Do you have a gun?"

The question was ludicrous. "I do not require primitive Earth weapons to protect my family."

She pulled her lips to the side and looked me over. "Okay. Well, after what happened earlier, we already know you can... you know... rock her world."

"I like rocks," Tanner said and Lucy laughed.

"It would be helpful if she were here," I added, feeling

the pang of longing. While I was making progress with her friend and her niece and nephew were now under my care, Olivia was the one I craved. "Tell me more about the... about where my mate is now. Why is she not with the children?"

"It is something she will have to tell you about. I don't know all of it, but it's something someone of your... size and background could help. Trust me, the kids are better off here." She covered her mouth, hiding a tired yawn. "She'll be really, really happy to see you when she gets home. Shocked but happy."

"You think so?" I asked, my turn to be wide-eyed, hope warring with the hurt and confusion I'd felt when she ran from me. She *ran*. As if I had hurt her. Scared her. I had been so careful, my beast reveling in her scent, her softness, her soft cries of pleasure. "She ran from me. I am afraid that I may have frightened her." I couldn't bring myself to say that I may have caused her pain. Could not force myself to even speak the words.

Lucy shook her head. "She wasn't scared. Trust me. You took her by surprise. Heck, you took the whole world by surprise. She deserves a little Atlan attention." She lifted her eyebrows up and down in the same way Rachel had earlier on the comms call. Tanner giggled, which made Emma do so as well.

"What is she like? Tell me everything you know about Olivia. I must know about my mate," I said eagerly.

She waved her hand back and forth in front of her as if swiping away my words. "Oh no. You need to ask her yourself. But I can say, whatever you did earlier, do it again. And again." She winked at me.

"Nack! Nack!" Emma said, clapping her hands.

Lucy narrowed her eyes at Emma. "You, little munchkin, should be in bed, not having a snack."

"Brock-we!" Tanner added, which made Lucy laugh.

"Fine. You stay with them, and I'll make some broccoli." Lucy left the room, and I assumed she was now in the Earth kitchen. This was a primitive planet and didn't have S-Gen machines and therefore required an entire room to prepare food. I'd had several weeks to adjust to the basic style of living.

"Can you be a pretend woof, like your name?" Tanner asked. Since he was still standing on my thigh, we were almost eye to eye.

I picked up both children as I stood, went into the center of the room and spun around in a careful circle. They giggled. Then I dropped to the ground to lay on my stomach and let them climb all over me.

I would enjoy the play of the children until Olivia returned. Then I would give them back to Lucy so that I could court my mate and hopefully get her up against a wall once more. My beast liked the idea.

"Woof!" Emma said and climbed onto my back.

livia

THE BAR'S entrance wasn't on the street but down a dark, nasty alley that reeked of garbage, piss and cigarette smoke. It was like every other shithole Jimmy Steel had made me walk into. I knew he sold drugs at better establishments than this. Upscale restaurants downtown. Salons. Spas. Anywhere people with money were used to getting what they wanted. That was the way the world worked. How it had always worked.

I had figured, after my second "job" for Jimmy the Asshole, that he sent me to places like this because he enjoyed getting me dirty. I looked so sweet and innocent on the outside. It was true, appearances were deceiving. I did everything I could to live a simple, uncomplicated life because the alternative—this—was never going to happen.

Then there was my brother and the rest of my fucked-up family.

There was a reason Lucy was with the kids and not one of the dozen cousins I had in this city. My family, or what was left of them, was toxic. Top to bottom. Drugs, mostly. Alcohol. Affairs. Drama. Always some kind of drama. Infighting. Fistfighting. Someone was always in jail or recently getting out.

I'd had enough. And Greg's kids, my babies, Tanner and Emma? They weren't getting near any of this. I'd break the cycle of misery and destruction so they wouldn't be tainted. Ever. So I'd cut my family off, every single one of them, after Greg died. No contact. New cell phone. New house. I cut out the cancer that had killed my brother, and I'd been happy. Until Jimmy came knocking and pulled me right back into the mess.

The door I had to knock on was covered in rust and cracked gray paint. The light on the corner, at the end of the alley, was out. Of course. I'd bet anything there were no working security cameras back here either. I pulled the diaper bag higher on my shoulder as if it would protect me.

Using the side of my fist, I banged on the door, hard, and hoped I wouldn't need a tetanus shot. The music coming from inside the dive bar was so loud I was afraid no one would hear me pounding.

I was wrong. The door opened slowly, and a large, tattooed bouncer looked me over from head to toe with something in his eyes I did not like. He was big but flabby. Greasy hair hung down over his forehead, and he needed to shave his jowls. He looked like an ugly, deflated version of Wulf. While I hadn't been scared of Wulf, I was definitely afraid of this guy. He had zero honor.

"I have a package for you," I said, not wanting to stand around and chitchat. The sooner I did this, the sooner I could be out of here.

"Yeah, sweetheart? I've got a package for you." He cupped his crotch and thrust his hips in my direction. His laugh made my stomach churn, but I stared him down even though I was a foot shorter. It was best not to show an ounce of reaction to these guys. If they saw me cower, they'd pounce on it. I'd learned that when I was six or seven.

Without a word I walked past him and into the back room of the bar. I'd been here before and went directly to the small office behind a series of iron bars. I didn't know who was back there, and I didn't want to know. The only thing I wanted to do was drop off Jimmy's drugs and get the hell home. Debt paid. Time served. This was the last one. With this drop I'd paid back my brother's debt to Jimmy Steel in full.

I reached into Emma's diaper bag and, from the inside pocket, pulled a package wrapped in thick brown paper and duct tape. I'd weighed every one Jimmy gave me. This one was the largest. Eight pounds of what? I had no clue. Didn't want to know. I was done.

D.O.N.E. *Done.*

Placing the package on the small shelf, I slid it under the bars until a pair of hands appeared to pull it out of my grasp, but I held on. Tight. I'd learned this lesson the hard way as well. "I want a receipt," I said.

The voice that answered sounded like half a pack of cigarettes and zero patience. "I'll let him know you delivered."

I shook my head. "Not good enough. I want a receipt."

The sigh was followed by a large belch, as if that would dissuade me. Try again. "No one double-crosses Jimmy. He's got connections, yeah? You cross Jimmy, you die, and no one goin' looking for the body, yeah? Don't you know who he is?"

"I know who he is." He was a drug dealer, a ruthless bastard who had made my life a living hell. That's who he was. I was done. "I still want a receipt."

"You don't know shit." A few moments later he slid me a business card with the bar's name on the front, a date, time and initials on the back. "Good enough?"

My answer was to take the card, let go of the package and walk out the back door like my hair was on fire. Tattoo Guy didn't bother speaking to me this time. I wasn't interested, and he had a job to do, which wasn't me.

I practically ran back to my car and drove home by rote memory, not remembering how I got there once I pulled into the driveway. I rested my head on the steering wheel and tried to catch my breath. Just breathe. It was over. I had done it. Paid Jimmy back, not been caught by the police, kept the kids safe. We could have a real life now. Quiet. Peaceful. No drama. No criminals. I was free. I smiled to myself, and for once it was real. Whole.

I needed a shower to wash it all away. God, every time I did this, I felt filthy, as if I hadn't bathed in days despite the shower I'd hurried through before I left. I hated using the diaper bag, but Jimmy had insisted. Now? I was going to throw it out, get a new one. I didn't want to touch that bag ever again, as if I were tainting my little niece by connection alone. Fear was exhausting. The closer I got to the different drop spots, the more I would sweat. A cold panic coated my skin. I only felt relief when I was back in my car and driving home.

It had been thirty minutes since I left the latest shipment, and the adrenaline was fading, leaving me restless and nauseated. The last drop, Jimmy Steel's guy had been forty minutes late, not giving a shit that I had two kids who'd wake me up at the crack of dawn for breakfast. All he cared about was me doing what I was told.

Greg had been gone a year. Besides having to adjust to an instant family, I'd had to deal with an instant blackmailer because I'd inherited his drug debt. Sure, I'd had nothing to do with it, but Jimmy Steel had come calling one night. Personally. I had to pay off twenty thousand dollars, allowing me to give him a mixture of my hard-earned income and delivering drugs for him.

All because of Greg. My brother had been in the military and deployed to Afghanistan twice. His wife, Sally, had raised the kids alone while he was gone. He came home whole in body but not in mind. Because our family was so screwed up, he'd gone the way of many others, followed their example and gotten into drugs to dull his mind. With it brought the debt.

I looked more like a soccer mom than mule, and I had a feeling that was why Jimmy'd used me. I was able to get away with it. For the past year. God, my nerves were shot. Thankfully Lucy watched the kids for me. There was no way in hell I was taking two toddlers to a seedy bar to deliver cocaine or ecstasy tabs or whatever was in those packages. So I'd lied and I was still lying to my best friend.

More like she was allowing me to lie to her. Which I very much appreciated. The less she knew, the better.

I hated Greg for this. Then I hated myself for hating him. He'd *died* and I felt so guilty for it. But why did he have to get in bed with a guy like Jimmy Steel? He could have come to me. To the doctors for help. Drugs, but good ones. Legal ones. But no. I was paying for his crimes.

Because of that, I felt tainted, like right now as I sat in the driveway. I was used to being *good*. I felt physically ill knowing I was helping put drugs into the hands of people who ruined lives. People probably *died* because of these pills. Or did stupid things that ruined their lives. I had to wonder how many were in debt to Jimmy like Greg had been.

I didn't think he'd ever done drugs... or at least I liked to think not. He'd come home messed up and made bad choices. Choices I paid the price for.

Not anymore. I was finished. When I'd left, Tanner was chattering away to Lucy from his bed. While both he and Emma should be asleep now, it was possible they were up again. I knew Lucy would let them stay up late, eat ice cream and generally run around like wild animals. They loved their nights with her, and I couldn't deny any of them the happy memories, even if it messed with their sleep schedule and they'd be cranky the next day. Lord knew those kids needed more of them.

So I glanced in the rearview mirror, fixed my hair. For being so young, Emma and Tanner were really observant. They picked up on when I was happy or sad, if I'd had a bad day. I'd fake it till I made it with them. I fake smiled at myself, then rolled my eyes and climbed from the car. Grabbing the diaper bag out of the back seat, I checked to make sure it was empty, opened the lid of the small trash can by the garage and threw it inside with the rest of the garbage.

I opened the door, half expecting sugar-induced whoops and hollers and being almost knocked down by leg hugs. Instead the house was super quiet as I stepped inside. I set my purse and keys down on the table beside the door, then turned and froze.

My heart leaped into my throat at the sight. There on my

old, worn couch was Warlord Wulf, asleep. On top of him, like two cute leeches, were Emma and Tanner, also asleep. Emma was spread eagle on his chest, Tanner tucked under one arm, his head resting on his ribs.

"Oh my God," I whispered when I felt my ovaries explode. *This* wasn't in any of the show's clips. I had no doubt if it were, there would be a line out the door for bride volunteers.

Asleep, Wulf's body was relaxed. No tense muscles. No stern looks. No clenched fists. Just... softness, although I'd never tell a seven-foot warlord he was soft.

What was he doing here, and why was he covered in kids?

Clearly he'd been here for a bit. There were toys on the floor, as usual. The coffee table was turned sideways, although I could see it was so his long legs could stretch out. If he'd put them on the table, I wondered if it would have broken.

Lucy came out of the kitchen and held a finger over her lips.

Yeah, no duh. I didn't want to wake them.

I tiptoed past, down the hall and into my bedroom. Lucy followed and shut the door behind her.

"I hate you so much," she whispered.

My heart was pounding so hard I figured she could see it. Warlord Wulf was here for me. Here! For me!

"What is he doing here?" I whispered right back even though I'd told myself the reason.

"He's here to *do* you."

I rolled my eyes.

"How did he even know where I lived?" I set a shaky hand on my chest. "Or who I am?"

89

She huffed out a laugh. "Are you serious? They tranqed him to keep him from following you. You think he'd stay away? Finding an address was not going to be an issue for him."

"What did you tell him? Where did you say I was?" I asked in a rush. What if he found out where I'd been? What I'd been doing?

Her eyes narrowed. "That you had something to do."

I was going to get struck by lightning. Smote. Something bad because yeah, I'd lied to my BFF to deliver drugs.

"That's it?" I practically squeaked. "He didn't ask any questions?"

"Oh, he asked questions. Would it have done him any good?"

No. That was the answer. Bless Lucy. She'd let me do what I needed to do. And now? I was free of Jimmy—*and* I had a hot alien sleeping on my couch who... was... here... for... me.

"Well, just so you know, that was the last time I had to volunteer."

She narrowed her eyes farther. "Right."

"What do I do about Wulf?" I kept my voice down so none of them woke up. I needed a minute. Okay, two. I wrung my hands. Bit my lip.

I had an alien on my couch. An alien I'd had sex with a few hours ago. An alien who said I was his mate.

"Have sex with him, you dummy. Oh, wait, you already did that." She grinned and I blushed.

"I have two little kids. How is that even possible? God, how do parents make a third child? Do they hide in the closet or something?"

Shrugging, she opened the bedroom door behind her. "You'll find a way. I know I would."

She slipped out, and I followed her to the front door. When I closed it as quietly as possible behind her and turned around, Wulf was staring at me.

He was awake.

I stared. He stared. He stared some more. Slowly and with a care I never expected someone of his size to have, he lifted Emma off his chest and set her gently on the couch beside him. Then he moved his arm out from under Tanner and also laid him down. I winced, since Tanner would surely wake up. But he didn't. I had to hope he was just plain exhausted from staying up late and having an Atlan to play with.

I swallowed hard as he stood to his full non-beast height. Here, in my little house, I realized how large he was. The bride program center was huge and had made him appear big, but not like this. He must have ducked through the front doorway when he came in.

He didn't say anything, only looked me in the eye as he took me by the hand and led me down the hall, just like Lucy had.

This was Wulf, not Lucy. My heart wasn't in my throat now, but I was tingly all over. Just our fingers touching gave me a zing. I was panicked but calm. Excited but... at ease.

I knew this guy. Well, I knew him when he'd been in a rage before, when he'd been a beast. He was chill now, as if his beast didn't need to come out. He knew who I was. Knew he was where he wanted to be.

I didn't understand it, personally, but the concept made sense now, especially since Lucy had updated me to what had happened on the show after I'd left.

He ducked through the bedroom doorway, and I closed the door behind me.

"Are you... are you all right?" I asked him. Just like

earlier, I tipped my voice low. "I heard they tranquilized you."

"You left me," he replied.

I felt like shit now. This huge alien was also a softy, and it seemed I had hurt him. I had no idea how that was possible, but it felt that way.

"I'm sorry. That was pretty crazy with everyone barging in and the cameras. I mean, it was on TV."

"It was not optimal, but I do not care where we are as long as we are together."

My mouth fell open. Had he just said that? He'd known me for, what? Fifteen minutes? Most of that time had been spent... yeah. Not going to go there right now, although my body wanted to desperately. It was as if my body'd had some Atlan cock and was addicted.

"Be mine, Olivia Mercier. Go to New York with me. Accept my mating cuffs."

"Are you asking me to... to *mate* you?"

He nodded. "I have made it very clear how I feel for you. How my beast knows you anywhere. You belong to us. I can't live without you."

I'd dreamed of a man saying that to me. *I can't live without you.* But men on Earth don't mean that literally. Wulf did. If he didn't claim a mate, he would die from mating fever.

I stared up into Wulf's face. "That's crazy. I'm not... I can't be your mate."

He frowned. "Why not?" he asked with a little snap to his voice. I was ruining his calmness.

I frowned back. "Why me? I mean... you had twenty-four gorgeous, friendly women to be your mate."

He shook his head adamantly. "My beast didn't desire any of them."

"It desires me?" I asked, tossing up my hands, completely confused.

"I think that was made obvious. Do you need a second demonstration? I will be more than happy to provide one for you."

Oh yes, I did. I *so* did. But that wasn't the point.

"Wulf, look at me." I lifted my hands and waved them in front of my body. "All of me."

He did. His dark gaze raked from my booted feet to the top of my head. I hadn't dressed up to go on the little errand for Jimmy Steel, but I didn't look like a slob either. Boots. Jeans. A dark T-shirt. This was my don't-be-seen-by-anyone-and-blend-in outfit and one that covered more skin than was required in Florida.

"I am."

"I'm... I'm not a small woman. Surely you want someone taller? Not so big? I can't compete with Genevieve and Willow. You should want them. They look like models and... you're... gorgeous." There, I said it, and his dark eyes turned to pools of near black as if I'd pleased him. "You could literally get any woman on this planet to fall at your feet. You should be with a model or an actress or something. Someone beautiful."

"I do not desire those females," he countered, then frowned. "You are very beautiful. You disagree? Are you saying I'm supposed to want human females who are angles and bones, like Woocy... I mean Lucy?"

I had to bite back a laugh at the name. Score one for Tanner. But this was serious. Men like him did not go for women like me. I was not even close to the feminine ideal. I'd been fat shamed since middle school. This could not be happening to me, not when he'd had two dozen of the most

93

beautiful women I'd ever seen all over him for the last three weeks.

"I think you made a mistake," I repeated.

He shook his head slowly as his heated gaze continued to rove over me. "You are soft. Everywhere."

I nodded. Now he was catching on. No amount of cardio was going to fix what I had going on. Not that anyone could tempt me onto a treadmill. I'd rather eat nails than volunteer for that kind of torture. I liked to breathe real air and not be in pain. If I wanted to eat a cookie, I was going to eat the damn cookie.

"They are too small." He held up his hands so I could see the size of them. "Brittle. I would break them."

I laughed at that, thinking of him in his beast mode trying to fuck Willow. Okay, that wasn't a good idea because I was jealous. Bad thoughts!

"Your thighs are thick, and I gripped all that soft flesh as I licked your pussy. I held you up with my hands on your wide ass, cupping it in my palms as I pressed you against the wall and pounded into you. I haven't yet, but I am eager to bury my face in your lush breasts and get lost."

"Oh my God," I whispered to myself as I stepped away from him but bumped into the closed door. I was wet and horny all over again. He was like a romance book on tape. I could listen to him talk about having sex with me for hours.

"I... well, okay. More sex sounds amazing and all, but... I'm not wearing your cuffs."

He took a step closer, and I tipped my chin back to meet his gaze.

"You're my mate."

Slowly I shook my head. "Impossible."

He stilled. "You do not believe me."

I wasn't going to shake my head again, so I stayed silent, pressed my palms against the door.

"I am not here because of the *Bachelor Beast*. There are no cameras. No Chet Bosworth."

I huffed a laugh at that. I could only imagine the commentary that megalomaniac would say if he were here, like a sports announcer doing a play-by-play as he peeked out of my closet.

"I shall show you."

He lowered his head to mine. Slowly, eyes opened. I watched his movement and knew the kiss was coming. This time, the beast wasn't in control; it was Wulf who was doing the kissing. He was able to speak in full sentences, able to control his breathing. Everything.

I didn't deny him because my body screamed *yes!*

We could figure out the whole mate thing after. Sex now, talk later.

His lips met mine at the same moment his hand curled around the back of my neck. His touch was gentle, his skin warm against mine.

And his lips... gentle, too. Almost coaxing.

I whimpered at the contrast to how he'd kissed me earlier.

"The kids..." I whispered against his lips.

He didn't say anything, only moved his hand to the door handle, turned the lock. It wouldn't keep someone like Wulf out, but it could deter two little kids long enough for me to throw some clothes on.

He kissed me again, his tongue flicking against my closed lips, and I parted for him.

I had no idea how long we stood there and kissed like teenagers, but I was lost to it. When he peppered the kisses down my jaw to my ear, I angled my head to give him better access.

"No mating. Just sex," I said, then let all thoughts disappear.

8

 ulf

SHE DID NOT BELIEVE ME. Even as I nuzzled her soft skin and fought my beast with every ounce of will, my mate refused to surrender to me, refused to see her own worth, her beauty. Refused to believe I would not survive without her.

I kissed her softly, gently, because if I let go, the beast would consume me. Her. Both of us. We'd fucked with the beast in control the first time. I couldn't savor, couldn't learn what made her hot or gasp or moan. Now I could. I wanted to take my time with every lush curve. To explore the softness of her breasts and generous hips. I wanted to feel her body melt beneath mine as I took her.

So I fought with myself, with my beast, even as I tried to woo her. *Go slowly.* Warden Egara's warning was clear in my mind. This was new for my female. Not sex, but the depth of our newfound bond. She had not been looking for a mate. She did not volunteer.

According to Earth laws, she was not mine, which made a rumble escape my chest.

When she tilted her head to the side and gave me access to her vulnerable neck, I nearly growled in both victory and hunger. She was mine. She was submitting to me. She would give herself to me, if I could control the beast.

"Wait."

That one word made my entire body freeze, my lips poised along the length of her jaw, my hands cupping her soft, round ass. I wanted to shove her against the door and make her cry out as she had earlier. But I held perfectly still.

"The kids," she said again. "We need to put them in bed. If they wake up in the living room alone, they'll be scared."

Her small hands pushed against my chest, and I stepped back, pleased that she cared so deeply for the children. She would be an excellent mother, and my beast calmed for the first time since her arrival. Content, as he had not been in years.

The feeling shocked me, but I did not attempt to rile him. We were protecting our own, ensuring their safety and well-being.

I simply followed my mate to the living room and lifted Tanner into my arms, careful not to wake him, as she carried little Emma to a small bedroom across the hall from hers.

Olivia's smile was soft and intimate in the dark room. The task of putting little ones to bed was a new experience for me, one I would crave in the future. This was the opposite of battle, of death and killing rage and blood-soaked horror. This was innocence and light, the reason warriors fought and died. This was life, not death, and I wanted more. Wanted her. Wanted a child *from* her.

Forever.

I laid Tanner on a small bed and pulled a blanket

covered with various animal designs of rabbits, puppies and kittens—soft, furry creatures that humans routinely kept as pets—over him. On the opposite wall stood an even smaller bed, the mattress barely reaching midcalf. Olivia placed Emma's head on the pillow, and the little girl snuggled into a fluffy blanket decorated with an odd assortment of drawn characters: a round bear wearing a red shirt, a very thin striped tiger who appeared to be able to speak, a grumpy looking rabbit and some kind of dark gray horselike creature whose ears drooped in a very pathetic fashion. Not even opening her eyes, Emma reached for a small toy animal, a copy of the red-shirted bear.

When Olivia saw me inspecting the strange assortment of creatures, she smiled. "Tanner loves animals. All animals. He says he wants to be a veterinarian when he grows up. And Emma—" Her smile made my heart melt even more for her as she reached down and ran fingertips over the little girl's forehead. "She loves *Winnie the Pooh*. As you can see."

I did not know what a *Winnie the Pooh* meant, but I said nothing, hypnotized by the expression I saw in Olivia's eyes as she looked at the two children. Her gaze grew rounder, soft. The worry lines disappeared, and her entire face relaxed into contentment.

Love. This was what love looked like on Olivia Mercier's face, and I hungered for that look to be directed at me. Needed it, more than I needed air to breathe, more than I needed to fill her with my cock and make her scream in pleasure, I needed her like this. Soft and gentle. Accepting and content. Loving.

Without a word I drew her close and held her for long minutes in the silence. She began to sway slowly, side to side, and I moved with her, stroking her back, my mind too full of what I had realized to express it with words, so I touched her instead, prayed to the gods that my hands, the beat of my heart beneath her soft cheek, would be enough. That she would know, sense in the mysterious way females seemed to grasp, what I was feeling, because I wasn't sure myself. It was too raw, too new to describe. To name. To control.

In the chaos of the *Bachelor Beast*, I'd found this moment of peace. When I'd transported from The Colony, I never expected to find this, a human of my own and children.

I couldn't stop the ache that filled my chest, but it was not the pain of a wound. This was different. Lingering. The ache spread, pain moving from my heart to my lungs until it hurt to draw air, up my throat, swelling there so that I could no longer speak, to my face, my eyes, where the pain pooled in the salty, unwelcome heat of unshed tears.

Even when captured by the Hive, I had not felt like this.

I did not cry, had never cried in living memory. Not since I was a very small child at my mother's knee. But I was helpless to stop them as Olivia's arms lifted to wrap around my waist and she leaned in to me, melted against me like she was exactly where she wanted to be. With me. Mine.

My beast sniffed, then settled, knowing the one female who belonged to us was in our hold. The children who belonged to her, and thus, belonged to me, safely asleep where I could watch over them.

Longing. That's what this was. Desperate, vulnerable longing. Longing to be part of her family, to be loved the way she loved these small human children, to finally matter to someone beyond what I could do on a battleship or to enemies in the war. I ached to be accepted as I was now, contaminated and damaged, barely in control of my beast. I longed to be hers. Just her. I needed a home, and she was that now, for me and for my beast.

I shuddered, the act instinctive and impossible to control. That betrayal of my emotions caused her to lift her head, to look up at me. Her gaze widened in shock. "Are you crying?"

"No." I was not crying. Salted water had overflowed my eye and tracked down my left cheek.

She lifted her hand and wiped the wetness from my face. "Why are you crying?" she whispered.

I shook my head, turned my face to kiss the inside of her palm. "You are so beautiful, mate. Too perfect to be real."

"I am not—"

I set a finger to her lips to silence her protest. I had already heard all she had to say about her perceived imperfections. She compared herself to other females, which was ridiculous. It was only my opinion on the topic that mattered, and I told her again how I felt. "You are perfect. Beautiful. Soft. I will not hear otherwise, or I will place you over my knee and spank you for treating yourself so poorly."

She raised her brows at the threat, but there was laughter in her eyes. "Is that so?"

"Yes." I lowered my head and buried my face in the curve of her neck, breathed her in, grounded myself in her existence. "By the gods, Olivia, you are my everything."

She shuddered in my arms, and I wondered what emotion had caused the tremor, hoped she was feeling what I did. Longing. Need. Desire.

When she pulled away, I was distraught, until she reached out and took my hand. "Come on. Let's get out of here before we wake up the kids." Her voice was so soft I was thankful for my beast hearing.

I followed without question, as I always would, the realization both startling and frightening as the beast settled completely at her command. He had already decided he was hers. He had surrendered completely, and the lack of boiling aggression inside was shocking to my system.

Olivia closed the bedroom door behind us and led me back to the living room. I had no idea what she intended, and I was content to allow her to have her way so long as she didn't stop touching me. We could sleep. We could fuck. We could talk all night. I could hold her for hours and be content. I was hers.

I had said the words before, meant them at the time, but I did not fully understand the inescapable reality until this moment. Hers. She was not my mate. She was not mine. *I was hers.* I would protect her, fuck her, kill for her, protect her. HERS.

"Come here, Warlord."

She pulled me to the couch and indicated I should take a seat next to her. I settled into the cushions and held back a growl when she pulled her small hand free from mine. It would not do to frighten her with my needs. Well, it was too late for that. I'd been insane and insatiable earlier. She knew what she was getting, and she was still here.

I could overpower her, control this situation, but I needed to see what she wanted, how she craved it. She could lead, and I would follow her anywhere.

I was the weak one here, the needy. She was strong. Independent. Caring for two children that were not hers. Working and being the provider.

Alone. She was alone. Like me.

All the lights were out now but one small lamp on the opposite side of the room. The soft light cast an intimate glow on her face, as if she sat before a fire in the dark of night. "You are beautiful, mate."

Her eyes blinked slowly, but she did not turn away.

"Don't start with that, Warlord. I want to know why you are really here. What are you doing at my house? I'm not a bride. You aren't supposed to be with me."

My entire body shuddered as I held back the beast. Without her touch I struggled to remain in control, especially when she spoke such disagreeable words. Perhaps I was not as content as I had assumed. Another shudder passed through me, and my jaw tensed as I clenched my teeth, holding back the transformation.

"What is it?" She frowned, her eyes searching my face. "What's wrong with you?"

I did not wish to lie to my female, not when the truth was much safer. "My beast is not happy that you broke contact with us. I am having difficulty holding him back."

"What?" She scooted closer, her adorable nose scrunched in confusion. "You mean you want to hold my hand?" She reached out and took mine between her two small ones.

"He requires touch, mate," I explained. "He is not human. I am not human."

She gave a little laugh. "Oh, believe me, I know." Her tone held what I hoped was humor, but I didn't worry about it as her hands squeezed mine. The beast calmed. "Better?"

Perhaps a small untruth would do no harm here. "He would settle if you were to sit on my lap."

"I am too big for—"

Not wishing to hear her speak poorly of her luscious curves again, I simply lifted her onto my lap and settled the back of her head on my bicep so she would be able to look at me. I wanted to see her eyes, her lips. The rise and fall of her breasts. *Feel her.*

"Oh!" She wiggled a bit, but when my cock swelled

beneath her round bottom, she stilled, her breathing quickening. "I guess this is better."

"Much." I lifted my free hand and gently cupped the side of her neck, the side of her face. Using my thumb, I traced the outline of her lips. "You are perfect, and I need to kiss you."

"Okay."

I froze. If I kissed her like I had in her bedroom, I would want more. I told her that as well.

She smiled. "Yes, I'm well aware of that. I want it, too. You are lethal, Wulf."

"Yes, mate? Or no?"

Instead of responding with words, she lifted a hand and repeated my actions, stroking my neck and cheek, my lips. Her eyes darkened as she pulled my head down toward hers. "I think I need more kisses, too."

I allowed her slight strength to guide my lips to hers. When she was so close I could feel the heat between them, she whispered, "We should really talk first."

"Tomorrow, mate," I promised. "Tonight, we do this."

"I'm not your—"

I crushed her lips to mine, not wanting to hear the denial again. She was mine. My mate. I knew the truth, as did my beast. We simply needed to convince Olivia of our devotion, and I knew no better way than bringing her pleasure.

 *ulf*

THE KISS TURNED carnal as I took what she offered. Her mouth. Her tongue. Just her. Her taste, her feel, her breath.

She was in my lap, and I curled her, lifting her so I could stroke from the back of her knee, up her thigh, over her soft, round ass, the curve of her hip, her waist, the side of her breast. I devoured her as I petted, learned the feel of her softness more thoroughly, enjoyed the way her body conformed to mine, settling into me as if filling every missing piece with her warmth.

"Wulf, the kids." Her whisper barely carried, but I recognized heat in her voice, the lure of the forbidden. "What if they wake up?"

"Then you will need to be quiet when I make you come."

Her response was a very wicked and very feminine smile against my lips. "I can do that."

"Can you? You have offered up quite a challenge to my beast. We shall see."

Moving quickly, she turned to straddle me so that we faced one another. "Take off your shirt," she commanded. "Earlier, I didn't get to see you."

I chuckled, pleased that she was eager to claim what was hers, and pulled the shirt off in one swift motion. When my gaze returned to her, it was to find her staring as if transfixed. "You can't be real."

I looked down to make sure nothing was amiss. Unlike other fighters on The Colony, I had no visible integrations. I had plenty everywhere, but they were beneath the skin. Inside.

"I am very real." Grabbing each of her hands, I placed them flat on my chest. The heat of her touch soothed and enticed me in equal measure. "I am real and I am yours."

She shook her head as if to disagree, but her small hands moved and I leaned my head back to enjoy the first real touch of my female. The beast in me preened, eager to come out and play, to present himself to her, to be petted and touched and accepted. But I pushed him back with a ruthlessness that shocked me. He'd had his time with her against the door at the testing center. He'd fucked her. Claimed her. Made her run from us.

This time was mine. Her touch? Mine.

Her small hands roamed, and I soaked in the smallest flicker of her gaze, the breathless sound of her excitement.

"I thought you had some kind of cyborg parts, but I don't see anything. Are the robot parts in your legs? Or somewhere else?" Embarrassment colored her cheeks, and she blushed a pretty shade of pink.

Slowly I shook my head, watched her. "No mate. I and a few others like me were contaminated with nanoparticles only. They live in my skin, in my muscle and bone. They are invisible to the eye but make me stronger and faster, harder to kill and better at killing."

She frowned as her eyes moved across my torso. "Invisible?" Her palm settled on my shoulder, and she traced the flesh there as if the idea fascinated her. "Why? I don't understand. Why would they change you at all? You're perfect. Why do you call yourself contaminated?"

Holding her gaze so I could gauge her reaction, I laid bare my shame. My failure. My defeat. If she could not accept this, she would not be able to accept me. "I fought many battles against the Hive. Too many to count." I took a breath, then continued. "But the last battle, myself and a small number of other Atlan warlords were captured."

"I'm so sorry." She leaned forward and placed a kiss in the center of my chest. I struggled to breathe, and it was a long moment before I could speak.

"Most Atlans resist the Integration Units, the Hive scientists who transform captured fighters into their newest foot soldiers."

"That sounds like some nightmare out of *Star Trek*. You know, like the Borg."

I had been asked about these fictional creatures within a few days of my arrival on Earth and had used their primitive computers to research the creatures about which she spoke. I shook my head.

"No. I have seen this television fiction and the creatures you call the Borg. The Hive is much more advanced. They do not clunk around on big square spaceships and recharge like batteries stuck in a port. The Hive integrates with biological material on a cellular level. There are no attachments or gadgets. The Hive become what they consume, which are Coalition fighters they capture. As I have now become Hive. That is why the integration of fighters is referred to as contamination. Most of the Hive technology becomes part of us. It cannot be removed. Mine is not visible, but it is there."

She squeezed my shoulder. "Does it hurt?"

So much for not talking. No matter how much I wanted her lips back on mine, this was what she wanted, my words, and I'd give them to her. I'd give her anything.

"Not anymore." I would not share with her the agony of the process as they'd dripped microscopic invaders into my bloodstream for hours on end. The agony and fire in nearly every cell in my body as the Hive pieces tore me apart on the cellular level and healed me again with new particles in place of the old. Hive particles.

"I still don't understand." A frown marred her forehead. "You escaped. You look normal. Why can't you go home to Atlan? Why do all those poor veterans end up banished to this Colony place?"

Her hands traced a line from shoulder to waist, the innocent touch appearing to me a mindless caress on her part. For me, it taunted the beast, and my cock swelled nearly to bursting. My female sat in my lap, her legs spread wide, her voice and her touch soft and welcoming. Every cell in my body wanted to rip her clothing off and plunge deep. But not yet. Not yet.

I grabbed her hands to still them, settled them over my heart. "The Hive technology also infiltrates the mind. On The Colony, we are protected from their communication frequencies. Deep within Coalition-controlled space as well. We are a danger to our people, always at risk of falling prey to the Hive's influence once more. That is why most of us do not choose to go back to our homes."

"But you can? If you want to?"

"Yes. We can now, since Prime Nial mated to a human female from Earth, a female who was also a soldier. She convinced him to change the law, that the risk was worth it to allow us to return home. Prime Nial himself is a contaminated warrior."

"So why don't you go home?"

"I am a danger to my people, Olivia. I seem calm at the moment, under your touch. But the beast lingers below the surface, ready to burst forth and fight, or fuck, at any moment. I can't always control him."

She was blushing again and bit her lower lip. "I know."

I tensed instinctively. "Did he hurt you?"

She turned bright red, and I became even more concerned. I could not live with myself if I'd harmed her in any way.

"No."

Within me, the beast chuckled as the smell of feminine arousal flooded my senses. I released her hands and placed mine on her waist. I needed her skin. Her softness against me. I needed to bury my cock inside her wet heat. I'd told her everything. She knew who and what I was, and she wasn't afraid, wasn't walking away. "Does he frighten you?"

"No."

Thank the gods.

"I want you again, Olivia. I want to bury my cock in your body, give you pleasure. I need to feel your skin. I need you. Now."

She shuddered as I had earlier, the tremor moving from her shoulders outward to her extremities. She lifted herself onto her knees and leaned forward to kiss me softly. Pulled back so that her answer was a whisper of heat over my lips. "Yes. I want you."

Moving quickly, I lifted her from my lap to stand before

me and stripped every bit of clothing from her body until she stood bare and beautiful in the light of one dim lamp. Every lush curve, every inch of pale skin was on display. Earlier I had not seen all of her. Only her legs, her creamy thighs, her pink, wet center. "You are beautiful, Olivia."

"Shhh." She stepped forward and placed her finger over my lips. "Strip, Warlord. If I'm naked, you're naked."

With a grin I lifted my hips from the couch and yanked my pants down past my knees. Making quick work of my shoes, I kicked the pants free and pulled her forward into a kiss.

She melted into me, her softness like nothing I had ever experienced in my life. I had fought and raged, pushed my muscle and bone to the breaking point in battles of both willpower and brute force, bone crushing bone. This was utterly different.

Olivia was softness and acceptance. Every part of her molded to me like a warm blanket. There was no struggle, no war, only comfort and pleasure. Divine, feminine seduction. Every touch made me want more. The heavy fall of her breast in my hand, the scent of her wet welcome, the hunger in her kiss. The catch in her breath, the quickening of her pulse.

My beast growled, threatened to rise, and I could not kiss her mouth, fuck her with tongue and cock and maintain control. Lifting her, I turned her to face away from me, the hard line of my cock sliding beneath her wet core as I settled her back to my chest.

"What are you doing?" she asked, trying to look up at me.

She did not protest as I placed her legs outside of mine and opened her pussy for my eager fingers. I stroked her thighs first, teasing her, enjoying the way her chest rose and fell as she panted with lust. I could look down at every inch of her.

"Try not to wake the children, mate," I warned. Finally she was bare and open and receptive.

With that as my only warning, I pulled one nipple as I plunged two fingers deep inside her pussy, working her clit with my thumb as she arched her back with a soft cry.

"Shhh," I murmured in her ear. "Can you handle this? Should I stop?"

Was that playful voice mine? I had not heard that tone before, at least not for so many years that I had forgotten it existed.

"Don't stop." She leaned back and turned her head, tried to reach my body with her lips. I did not need that level of distraction. This was my time, not the beast's. If he rose, I would be on my feet and Olivia would be pinned to the door. The wall. Bent over the kitchen table as he rutted into her like the wild animal he was. I wanted her like this. On my lap, legs spread wide. Open. Accepting. Every inch of her melding with every part of me.

"Lift your arms, Olivia. Wrap them around my neck."

She did as I bid without hesitation, and my beast preened at her submission to us.

I worked her clit, sliding my fingers in and out of her pussy until she clenched down to orgasm, then denied her. Over and over until she was writhing on my lap, begging.

Keeping one ear focused on the children—as I would tease my mate but never embarrass her should they stir—I lifted her and placed her wet core over my cock.

"Yes. Do it. God. Do it." She wiggled and I allowed her to move, to lower herself down on me, stretching her open, filling her. Completing her.

When I bottomed out, her pussy clamped down like a

fist, and I bit back a groan of my own as her mouth opened on a silent scream.

———

OLIVIA

SO FULL. So tight. So incredibly tight.

His hands were everywhere. On my clit. Playing with my nipples. Gently placed across my throat in a way that made an inner naughty Olivia light on fire like a blowtorch.

The orgasm ripped through me as he filled me. Thick. Hard. So big. So mine.

My pussy was still swollen from earlier, from the door, from his beast. And now he was behind me, the angle of his cock inside me so direct. So deep. I was splayed out like an offering on his chest, and I loved it. Fucking loved it.

He pumped his hips up and into me once. Twice.

The tension spiraled, my moan impossible to constrain within my throat as my pussy rocked into spasms again. I'd thought what we'd done earlier had been amazing, but this... a completely different side to Wulf.

"Come, mate. Come all over my cock," he ordered as his hand rested on my throat, a gentle but possessive touch that made me feel both vulnerable and safe at the same time. His opposite hand rubbed my clit in a rhythm that made me whimper as he fucked me. Hard. Fast. Slow. Deep.

I came again. My pussy was so swollen and sensitive that squeezing my inner muscles kept me awash in pleasure.

"Wulf." His name lingered on my lips as his heat flared at my back. My pussy spasmed hard, the jolt of my orgasm making my toes curl and my heart race until I couldn't breathe. "Wulf."

I didn't know what I was asking, only that I needed. More. Less. Him.

"Mate."

His touch gentled, the hard demands of his cock changing into a soothing tempo that felt like a caress. Like care. Tenderness. Was this love? Was this what making love felt like?

I had never been in love. Not once in my life, so I didn't know. All I knew was this was bliss and I'd only known him a few hours. He'd known instantly that I was his. Was there something in me, some instinct, that knew he was mine in return? Could it be possible?

His hands gentled as well, the roughness of his palms moving over my skin with reverence. Maddeningly slow. Every movement a soft and deliberate exploration.

I slid my fingers up over my head and into his hair and held on as he worshipped me. His cock filled me in a gentle glide that felt like it could go on forever.

"Wulf." This time his name sounded like a prayer, and I was glad he could not see my face.

"So soft. So beautiful. So perfect. By the gods." He groaned, his cock swelling as he fought not to come inside me.

"Yes." I squeezed him with my inner muscles, deliberately pushing him closer to the edge of his own release. I wanted him to feel as I did. "Come inside me."

With a shudder he moved his hand to my clit and stroked gently at first, then faster and faster as he increased his own pace.

He held on until I exploded again, my body on the brink

of complete exhaustion. I knew my pussy would be sore, and I didn't care. I never wanted it to end.

His hot seed filled me and the sound he made bordered on pain and I reveled in the knowledge that it was me—*me!* —that had brought him such pleasure. I'd made him like this.

He said he was mine, whispered it to me as we settled, as the sweat on our skin began to cool, our breaths evening out. Long minutes later he carried me to bed and climbed in with me, settling at an angle for the best fit. When he pulled me into his side, I snuggled there like he was mine. For tonight I would pretend, even if I knew I couldn't keep him.

10

TODAY... God, today was like a dream, right from the very start. I'd fallen asleep in Wulf's arms. Actually I'd fallen asleep on top of him because my bed was too small for his incredible size. He'd slept at the diagonal, but even then his feet hung off the bottom. His body was like a furnace. The air-conditioning was going to get a workout. Since we'd trashed the bed with our wild lovemaking, we'd slept with only the sheet on top of us, untucked. The rest of the bedding was strewn on the floor along with our clothes.

Maybe it was the orgasms. Maybe it was the fact that I was done with Jimmy Steel. Or maybe it was the protective embrace of Wulf's arms on me, but I slept hard and peacefully. Just after six, there was a rattle on the doorknob.

"Auntie! Why's the door locked? I'm ready for juice!" Tanner called.

"Me, too!" Emma shouted directly after.

I startled, remembering myself. I was naked on top of a naked alien. Not the best situation to be in with toddlers. They'd ask questions, lots of questions. Then they'd tell everyone from the checkout clerk at the grocery store to Mr. Zajak down the street all about it.

Wulf hadn't panicked—perhaps because he wasn't familiar with the filter-free honesty of children—and kissed the top of my head. He got up to put on his pants. I wasn't a morning person, but I'd gotten used to the kids' early wake up. I was always amazed at how dang perky they were. It was as if their batteries had been recharged, their power at one hundred percent and they were raring to go again. I needed at least one cup of coffee to be functional.

"Auntie!" Tanner cried again, the handle jiggling some more.

Wulf looked down at me, and his gaze heated. He said nothing, only padded, shirtless, over to the door and opened it. His large body easily blocked the kids' view of me, for which I was grateful.

"What's this about juice?" he asked, ducking through the doorway and closing it behind him.

"Woof! You're here. Is Auntie asleep? Did you lose your shirt?" Tanner asked.

I could hear them walking down the hall, one heavy set of footsteps and the pitter-patter of two more. I took the opportunity of alone time to slip into a sleep shirt. I had no idea how long it would be before they barged in, but they would, and I wanted to at least have something on. I'd gotten them to learn about a closed bathroom door and privacy, so at least I was able to pee by myself now. But that solitude had yet to extend to my bedroom.

"I did lose it." Wulf's voice, while tempered to be soft, was easy to hear. "I think we're going to have to go on a search for it. After breakfast I'll teach you how to be Everian and hunt."

I was thankful the house was small and I could easily hear their conversation. I wanted to know how Wulf interacted with the kids. All I'd seen was them asleep on him the night before. It was so sweet it had me smiling.

Emma didn't remember her parents. She would never know anything about them other than what I shared or in a picture. Tanner remembered them, although the images would probably fade. Even so, Greg had rarely been around since he'd been deployed for most of Tanner's life. Neither had much of a male influence, and so they were soaking up Wulf's attention like little sponges.

"What's a 'verian?" Tanner asked.

"It's a person from a planet called Everis. They are very skilled at finding things."

"Like lost shirts?"

"Especially lost shirts because they are very important. I can't go outside without one."

"You'll get a sunburn," Tanner explained.

I covered my mouth with my fingers to stifle a laugh. The three of them talking—well, Tanner and Wulf, but I expected Emma to be listening to their every word—made my heart flutter. How could someone so big be so gentle? I thought of him with the kids but also with me last night. I knew he could be wild and passionate. Unleashed. Yet, he could be almost... reverent with me.

I heard cabinet doors opening and closing. "Where is the juice?"

"There!" Emma said.

"In this big box? It's cold inside. Interesting."

"Auntie!" Emma shouted.

"Auntie is tired. While the three of us played last night before she came home, your auntie and I played after you went to sleep."

My mouth fell open and I blushed, remembering exactly how we *played.*

"I wanted to keep playing," Tanner said, and I could hear the pout in his voice.

"It was her turn to play. As a little warrior, I'm sure you understand taking turns."

"I do," Tanner said.

"I do," Emma parroted.

"Good. I'm proud of you for that. Your auntie, she works hard and needs to sleep a little longer this morning. We can be thoughtful and be quiet for her."

I never told Wulf what I did for a living, but he had to know I was the provider for the kids.

"Shh!"

"That's right, Emma," Wulf praised. "Shh." I could see him putting his finger to his lips just as Emma liked to do.

I flopped back in bed, listening to the three of them, and closed my eyes, imagining what it would be like to have a Wulf of my own like this. He was... perfect. Kids were baggage. *Serious* baggage. Guys who'd expressed any kind of interest in me over the past year pretty much burned rubber to get away from me when they found out I had two kids to raise. Sure, there were guys out there who were decent and would take me and the kids on, but I hadn't found any of them.

Well, maybe I had, in Wulf. But wishes were like unicorns. They were pretty and all but never appeared.

I must've fallen back asleep because I stirred at the

sound of shuffling and whispers. Rolling to my side, I leaned over the bed and stared at three faces. All three of them were on their hands and knees and wore capes, Emma and Tanner with their favorite blankets tied around their necks. Wulf had one around his as well, a bedsheet with trucks on it, which I assumed he'd pulled from Tanner's toddler bed.

"Auntie!" Tanner said, popping up from his crawl. He had a juice-stained mustache on his upper lip. "We're 'verians!"

Emma jumped to her feet and stood beside him, grinning.

I took in their outfits. Rubber rain boots on their feet, the pajama legs tucked into them.

"Are those the curtain ties from the other room?" I asked. Tanner and Emma wore green bands that were over one shoulder diagonally like a sash. They matched what was on the window in the living room. Affixed to these sashes were paper clips that held square sticky notes.

Wulf stayed on his hands and knees, which made them all about the same height. He was looking at them with open adoration. I was looking at his bare torso with open adoration of my own. When he glanced up at me, heat in his gaze, I loved knowing he could be this caring with the children, then in private so bold. So wild. "Olivia, this is Senior Hunter Tanner and Hunter Emma."

Tanner patted the turquoise sticky note. "This is my Hunter belt and badge. It's written in verian!"

Emma squatted down and grabbed Wulf's shirt. "Found it! Me Hunter!"

"You did! You found it, Emma!" Tanner praised, patting her little shoulder, then passed the shirt to Wulf. "Why's it here in Auntie's room?"

Wulf sat down on his butt on the floor, untied the sheet-cape around his neck, then slipped the shirt over his head. Tanner and Emma launched themselves at him, and he tickled them until they squirmed and squealed, thankfully making Tanner forget his question. I smiled at the sight. Seeing the three of them together made me forget why I couldn't be his mate.

———

TWO HOURS LATER, after a requested lunch of grilled cheese and, oddly, broccoli, the kids were in their swimsuits out back and running through the sprinkler. Wolf and I sat in lawn chairs beneath the small covered patio as we watched. Even in the shade, sweat dotted Wulf's brow, and he used a kitchen towel to wipe his head.

"Is it hot on The Colony?" I wondered. I wasn't sure how he would tolerate Florida weather with his size.

He turned his gaze from the children to me. "You can't breathe the air there, so we live in a controlled environment."

"You don't go outside?" I asked, stunned.

"Each base is enclosed inside a dome. A bubble, I believe, is the English. It is not hot. Now Trion, a planet far from The Colony, is very hot in places. Desertlike and dry. You will like it there. Not Trion—well maybe you would, but I was referring to The Colony."

I reached for my glass of iced tea from the patio table to stall. A drip of cold condensation fell onto my thigh. "Um, I'm sure I would," I replied neutrally.

I knew The Colony was full of veterans from all planets within the Coalition, including Earth, who had been captured and tortured by the Hive. I didn't want to offend him by saying anything inappropriate about the place after all he and his friends had been through.

"When you wear my cuffs—"

"I can't wear your cuffs—"

We spoke at the same time. Stopped at the same time.

I sighed. "Wulf, I can't be your mate."

His body was tense again, not as if his beast had returned but as if he was not happy with my news. I didn't blame him, not after all he'd been through with the Hive and even here on Earth.

"You have said that yet offered no reason. I wish to hear it."

The kids squealed as they hopped over the hose, the sprinkler oscillating back and forth. They were drenched, and the grass was sodden. They were having fun without either of us having to participate, which was a win, because Wulf and I needed to talk.

I sighed, took a sip of my tea.

"Tanner and Emma. They are the reason I can't."

He frowned, watched the kids. The corner of his mouth tipped up when Tanner stuck his butt over the spray. "I do not understand."

"I can't go, not with kids. It's not allowed."

He finally looked at me, and I saw his dark eyes fill with confusion. "Yes, you can."

I shook my head. "No. I can't. The rules say a woman can't be matched if she has children. She can't leave them behind."

"I wouldn't ask you to. You are mine." He tipped his head toward the kids. "They are mine."

He wanted the kids? It was one thing for his beast to say, *Mine,* when it came to me, but the kids, too?

I opened my mouth to respond, but he cut me off when he set his hand on my thigh.

"You are not being matched. You are my mate. My beast has identified you as such. Therefore you will wear my cuffs. That makes you an Atlan mate, and you, along with any offspring you have, go where I go. I go to The Colony."

I stared at him, perhaps to see if he was lying, but also to think through his words. "Genevieve and Willow volunteered."

"They did. But my beast chose you. As soon as you put on the cuffs, when you accept my claim, you are mine and I am yours. By all laws, Earth's and the Coalition's, you become a citizen of Atlan. You become my mate. Tanner and Emma become my children. My family. We can leave immediately for the transport room. Once you are mine, the rules for Interstellar Brides no longer apply to you. You are the mate of an Atlan warlord. We do not leave our females and children behind. No one would dare ask."

"Ever?"

"Never. My beast would kill an army of Hive soldiers to protect you or the children."

I stared. And stared. I heard the kids in the background but couldn't focus. All I had to do to be with Wulf was put on the mating cuffs and all three of us could leave Earth?

"Just like that?" I asked.

"Yes, it is that simple."

He stood as if ready to go now.

"What about the show?" I asked.

He growled, then dropped back into his seat. "I have not forgotten the show. They have my mating cuffs in New York."

I frowned. "They're, what, holding them hostage?"

"I am not familiar with this term outside of battle, but

they are keeping them so that I can give them to you during the live program. Warden Egara said it was for promotion."

I couldn't help but laugh. "Of course, they have to get that happily ever after."

It was to be mine. A thrill shot through me—and scared the crap out of me. It meant going off with an alien I barely knew to a planet far, far away. Sure, I had wanted to volunteer in the past, but there hadn't been a real, live, breathing, gorgeous alien in front of me. I had the kids to think of now. Would they be happy in space? So I asked him.

"The children? Happy?" he asked. "Of course. There are several children on The Colony now. All have Earth mothers like you, and they are of similar ages. They will have friends, and they will be watched over and protected, raised by the entire base."

His adamance eased my concerns, but still... it was one thing to go to a far-off country on vacation, but this was starting a life on a new planet. It would be with Wulf and that... I wanted to do it. My gut wasn't telling me no. It was telling me *hell yes*. My head was the one screaming that I was crazy.

"Besides needing the cuffs on your wrists, it is important I leave this planet in a positive way so that females will volunteer to be matched to The Colony. It was the goal of this program to begin with and why I came. I will see that through, which means we must go to New York for an interview program. Warden Egara has informed me that we must make goo-goo eyes. Whatever that is."

I burst out laughing. "Do we have to do it onstage?" My mouth was suddenly dry, and I took a big swig of my tea. I wished it were stronger and heavily laced with alcohol. Goo-goo eyes and mating cuffs? This was becoming quite the show.

"Yes, we. The show is now about you and me. How my beast chose you. How we are... suited and ultimately mates with matching Atlan cuffs. The finalists will be there. It's something called a tell-all, although I have no idea what that is."

"Oh God." I closed my eyes, thinking of all the reality shows I'd seen where all kinds of dirt was dragged up. Sometimes it wasn't pretty. That meant... God, they were probably digging stuff up on me right now. Like my family. Greg. And...

"That's not a good idea," I told him.

"Why not?"

I explained what a tell-all was, how Chet Bosworth would share every intimate detail of our lives for the entire world to pick apart. "Do you have secrets you don't want shared?" I asked him.

He sat quietly, thinking. "I was matched to a volunteer bride from Earth several years ago, before Earth was granted membership in the Coalition. She was part of an exploratory team, sent to investigate the program before your government revealed the truth to the people of Earth."

"What?" All excitement about possibly being his fell away like petals on a dying flower. He'd been matched. Had he pressed her up against a door and taken her as he had me? "Where is she now?" I asked softly. "Did she die?"

His eyes flared wide. "Die? No. I believe she is alive and well. Married, as they say here on Earth. She took nineteen of her thirty days, then refused me and my beast. She said she'd made a mistake, left a man she loved on Earth and could not be mated to me."

What? There was a woman who didn't want Wulf? And they'd been matched through the testing program? The chances of that happening, where the match was bad, was less than one-hundredth of one percent. Wulf had almost better odds at winning the Powerball jackpot than having a tested mate reject him.

Yet he had.

"Well, I'm still sorry. That must have been painful for you." That woman, whoever she was, was an idiot.

"She is my only secret, although not much of one."

"You did not give her your cuffs?" I asked, wondering if the Atlan bracelets I'd seen onstage were hand-me-downs.

"She rejected me. She was not my mate. No cuffs. As for Ruth—that is her name—she is the only information of use they will find. The rest is about my service, my capture... nothing worth mentioning."

My mouth fell open. "Your service to the Coalition is definitely worth mentioning. You are a brave warlord. You survived the Hive in so many different ways. That is to be honored. Respected."

He offered me a small smile but said nothing. He was humble, too.

"Woof, watch! I'm a moose!" Tanner jumped through the sprinkler, but I had no idea how he looked anything like a moose.

"And you, Olivia? What secrets do you keep?"

My eyes widened. "I... um..."

"Where did you go last night? Lucy believes you need my help."

I pursed my lips at my friend's annoying blabbermouth.

"I can't speak of it," I said, telling the truth. Jimmy had threatened to harm the kids if I ever told anyone. While I might be done with my work for him, he still dealt in bad things—ha, a total understatement!—and I had no doubt he'd still go after Tanner and Emma if he felt so inclined.

"Can't or won't?" he asked.

I hated that he was perceptive.

"Can't," I replied. I shifted in my chair, crossed my arms over my chest.

He reached out with one hand and grabbed my chair, sliding it across the concrete to be directly in front of him so our knees bumped. His gaze met mine. Held.

"'Can't' means you are unable to do so for a reason. What is your reason?"

I licked my lips and he watched. It had been a year, and I hadn't told anyone about Jimmy Steel. About Greg's debt. Not even Lucy, and I'd wanted to do so on many occasions. One intense stare by an alien and I had my own little tell-all, right in the backyard.

"Because someone will hurt the children if I say anything."

Wulf's jaw clenched, and I thought of an alligator. All that power waiting to be unleashed.

"Who dares threaten my children?" The one word was like a whip, sharp and ruthless.

Taking a deep breath, I tried to wait it out. Maybe be interrupted by the kids with another moose demonstration.

"Olivia Mercier. I must know who will hurt Tanner and Emma so I can rip their heads from their bodies."

With that, I laughed. Hard. For the first time in a year I found Jimmy Steel funny. Funny enough that the humor in Wulf's words had tears streaming down my face, and then it turned into sobs. Yet he wasn't joking, and that was why I had waterworks of my own.

I covered my face with my hands and was scooped up to sit on Wulf's lap, his arms around me. I cried and cried.

"What's wrong, Auntie?" Tanner asked. "Got a boo-boo?"

"She has a boo-boo on the inside, Tanner."

"Kiss and make it better," he said.

"I will," Wulf promised. "I'll watch out for your auntie while you both play in the water. Show me this moose you spoke of once again. I am not familiar with it."

I heard the children squeal and splash as I rubbed my face into Wulf's hard chest and tried to stop the tears. They ended eventually, when there were none left. He'd done nothing except stroke his big hand up and down my back patiently.

"A poison must be bled from the body. Human females I've met on The Colony like to do as you did. Cry for a long time."

I didn't know these women on his planet, but I figured we would probably get along.

I sniffled and looked up at him. He was so big, so handsome. Rugged. Fierce. Yet he was holding me as if I were the most precious thing in the world.

"Are you ready now to tell me who is threatening the children?"

I wiped my cheeks with my fingers. "Jimmy Steel."

"Why is he a menace?"

"He... deals drugs. Prostitutes. Gambling. All kinds of bad things. My brother, Greg, owed him money."

I felt him stiffen beneath me, but he didn't move.

"If your brother is paying him, why does this Jimmy Steel threaten you?"

"My brother died last year, with his wife. The kids are his, and I became their guardian. I took on the kids, but Jimmy Steel said I had to take on Greg's debt to him."

"How?"

I looked to the kids, innocently playing.

"I was a drug mule. Someone who carried illegal drugs from one place to another."

"I am familiar with this. Quell is rampant in space ports all across the universe."

I'd never heard of Quell, but it didn't surprise me that outer space had some of the same issues we did down here on little planet Earth.

"Last night was my final delivery. We agreed to a certain amount of cash to pay off the debt, but the rest would be paid off delivering drugs. I'm finished with our agreement, with Greg's debt."

Wulf sighed. "I am pleased to know you won't associate with him any further. You are afraid this may come up in the tell-all program in New York?"

I shrugged. It was then I realized I was on his lap. Comfortable, sheltered. Protected. If anyone could keep the likes of Jimmy Steel away, it was Wulf. I almost laughed at the idea of him going with me the night before, seeing the bouncer's face at that seedy bar if Wulf stood beside me.

"My family will come up as well. They aren't nice. I don't associate with any of them anymore, but I have no idea if the producer went and searched them out, got them to talk about me in one of their clips."

"It matters not to me about what is shared on the program or how those on Earth respond."

"What about the other fighters? Won't their chances of finding a mate be less?"

He kissed the top of my head. "I would assume other females from Earth have secrets and they will find you relatable."

I had to laugh. "I highly doubt every woman has to pay off a debt to a drug kingpin."

"I will protect you and the children. It is now my job. The children will come to New York with us. Separation is not an option."

Separation is not an option.

"Especially when you have my cuffs upon your wrists."

God, those words. He held me close as we watched the kids, and I wondered if he'd even let me off his lap. I realized I was content exactly where I was. And the cuffs? Being bound to him in such a way? Maybe I was crazy, but I wanted it. I wanted him.

11

W *ulf, New York City*

I THOUGHT the weather in Florida was bad. I thought Chet Bosworth was bad. I even thought the human airplane was bad. But nothing, absolutely nothing could prepare me for New York City.

I'd grown up on Atlan. Yes, there was a large population on the planet and it even had cities, but Gods.

The buildings reached the sky. There was no greenery. No trees. Planets. Flowers. At least none that I'd seen. And it teemed with people. Noise. So much to look at, my head hurt. Nothing anyone could say to me would have made me believe reality. I was claustrophobic walking on the sidewalk, and I was over a foot taller than everyone around me. I could see in the distance and knew it went on and on and on.

The show had provided a vehicle to retrieve us from the airport. I wouldn't even talk about that experience. Flying.

As if! Humans had no idea what *real* air travel was like. This ground vehicle was spacious and more luxurious than any ground craft I'd seen in space. My legs could extend out long and not touch anyone. A small miracle.

The children had come, along with things called car seats that ensured their safety while traveling, a diaper bag for Emma, a toy bag for both children's entertainment, a suitcase of their clothes, plus drinks and snacks. I had no idea how two tiny humans could require so many things. It was good we had such a large vehicle to carry it all.

Lucy had been asked to join us, although by her excitement I doubted she would have said no to Olivia. She was glad to watch Tanner and Emma while we did the program. I was at ease by this request, for I knew how well she cared for them and would protect them in my absence. The producer had requested them to be on the program, but Olivia had been adamant and flat out refused having Tanner and Emma shown in any way. She'd said it was one thing for the two of us to have images all over the world, but the children hadn't asked for it and would remain anonymous.

The vehicle first went to the hotel where a representative of the show met us and assisted Lucy, Tanner and Emma to their room. Olivia had given out kisses and hugs to the children and waved as they entered the tall building, hand in hand with Lucy.

"You are not worried about being separated?" I asked, staring at the strange revolving entry. People swarmed around us, a haste in their steps as if they had somewhere important to be. I pulled Olivia close. It would be easy to lose someone in this chaos, and this was the last place I wanted my beast to come out. Lucy had mentioned something about Godzilla, a strange beast-like creature, and told me not to turn into it. At the time I didn't know what she meant, but now I did.

"Lucy will keep them safe," she said reassuringly. "They will check in and go right to the suite we've been given. They've been wound up with excitement for hours. They've never been on a plane before. I'm sure they'll conk right out... after jumping on the beds."

I frowned down at her and she laughed. "It's fun." The sound and her optimism soothed my beast. Ever since she'd shared her burden about the drug dealer, she'd been more relaxed. I wasn't. I wanted to find the fucker and have him spend some time with my beast. But vengeance was not going to happen. I'd rather have her and the children off planet so I knew they would be safe.

Earth was such a primitive planet with too many self-serving, malicious humans.

"It's all right," she said, pulling me from my thoughts. "Come on. Don't you want those cuffs?" Her words were meant as a taunt, but they were a clear reminder of what we had to do. While I had Olivia beside me, our relationship was not our own and couldn't be until this... tell-all program was complete and I had the mating cuffs on her. Although my mating fever wouldn't be soothed until I claimed her as my beast required. Up against a wall, her hands pinned over her head, my cock deep inside her as I took her hard and made her scream.

I growled at the thought, knew it wouldn't happen until we were off this forsaken planet and back on The Colony. My cock was hard, and I had to adjust myself to be comfortable in my Earth-tailored pants.

Her words and the thought of claiming her pussy as my own had me moving, pulling her along by my hand gently at her elbow, back to the large vehicle. As soon as the door was closed, she crawled onto my lap so she straddled me, rubbing her center over my hard length.

The driver was separated from us by a divider so we had complete privacy. The noise and bustle from outside was silenced. We were alone.

We'd shared a bed again last night but only for a few hours. Tanner had come in, wanting a drink of water, but then decided he wanted to sleep with us. While the boy was quite young, he needed to maintain some independence, especially during sleep. Therefore I told him warriors slept in their own beds, and I ended up sleeping on the hard floor in his room to ensure he remained there.

Olivia cupped my jaw in her small hands. "I can't believe I'm saying this, especially since I've known you such a short time, but I missed you last night." She bit her lip, and I reached out and tugged the plump flesh free with my thumb. "You only gave me one orgasm."

The smile on her face indicated she had a playful side, a side my beast and I liked in equal measure. My cock throbbed as I remembered how I gave her that orgasm. My hands settled on the curves of her ass, then slid down her thighs to the edge of her skirt, then right back up. This time I cupped bare skin and the silky material of her panties.

"Then you shall have a second orgasm." My fingers slipped beneath the edge of the dainty material to find her center. Wet, hot and ready for me. I might not be able to claim her until we were on The Colony, but I could satisfy her in the moving vehicle.

"Here?" she asked, her eyes falling closed.

My finger slid easily into her snug pussy. Oh yes, she'd go on camera with a flush from the pleasure I gave her. "Here. Now."

———

OLIVIA

I WAS USED to being on set. I was used to hair and makeup, the crazy pace of a television show. But I'd always been behind the scenes. No one used to notice me. Now I wondered if everyone could tell I'd been skillfully finger fucked in the back of the limo. Those who did my face and hair thankfully didn't comment that I had a very satisfied look about me.

Now I was the one on the stage, all dressed up in one of the show's cute contestant outfits, with the cameras focused on me. Sure, Wulf was the main interest of the show, but I'd been the reason for him going all beast. Everyone wanted to know about me.

The set wasn't as elaborate as the original show in Florida. There was a raised dais for us to sit on long sofas. I'd seen the program before, knew multiple guests were interviewed at once.

Behind us was the same glass display box as in Florida with a spotlight focused on the cuffs. A very visible reminder of what this show was all about.

Besides Wulf and I was Chet Bosworth. He seemed to have recovered from a destroyed microphone, because as soon as the red light came on over the camera, he grinned and gave it his all.

"Who thought, folks, that we'd be here? The Bachelor Beast has found his Beauty, but not as expected. Of course, the bachelor isn't human and is wildly unpredictable. Nevertheless we can't seem to get enough of our own Atlan beast and the woman he's chosen. Please welcome to the program Warlord Wulf and Olivia Mercier!"

The live audience clapped and cheered.

His mood switched to serious. "I must say, Warlord, that your behavior during the last live program was... intense."

Wulf sat next to me in a pair of black pants and a white dress shirt. I had to wonder if they were tailor-made for his huge size. He looked good in them, like he had in the tuxedo, but it was like trying to put a dress on a cat. Wulf was a warlord, not human, and would never be one, regardless of what he wore.

While we sat side by side, we were angled toward Chet.

Wulf looked to me and smiled. He took my hand and raised it to his lips. The gesture was sweet and seemed contrived. Was he doing everything he could for the program so he could get the cuffs, get the bride volunteers and get the hell out of here?

"I found my mate."

"Isn't that sweet, folks?" The audience clapped. "A man of few words."

Chet turned my way. "Tell everyone about yourself, Olivia."

I wiped my sweaty palms on my skirt and smiled. "Well, I'm a makeup artist who'd been working on the show. I was watching the final episode, and as you saw, Wulf... found me."

He leaned in. "Every woman in the world wants to know... how was he?"

My mouth fell open and I stared.

"The blush tells all!" he twittered. The audience laughed, and I wanted to run from the stage. "You have many, many enemies now that you've taken Wulf and are ending his bachelor days. Team Genevieve and Team

Willow have shared their disappointment as both contestants were in a dead heat right up until the end."

"Both women are very nice. They deserve to find their perfect mates."

"The question is, do they think you deserve yours? Let's find out right now!"

Chet stood and the crowd clapped.

"Let's bring out Genevieve and Willow, the show's scorned finalists."

Oh boy. I'd watched enough daytime talk shows to know what Chet was trying to do. Reality TV loved to pit people against each other, driving up conflict, forcing viewers to pick sides. To love and hate in equal measure. I had no interest in a catfight on-screen. Or, using Chet's analogy, I didn't have a horse in this race. It wasn't my fault Wulf chose me. I didn't intentionally *take* him from either of them.

He. Chose. Me.

The women came out onstage, waving and smiling at the camera. Instead of fancy dresses like the other night, they had on cute, casual outfits. Their makeup was perfect, and I wondered who had done it. No bright pink lipstick in sight. They took seats next to each other on the far side of Chet so he was in the middle between all of us.

"Welcome, ladies. I'm sure you've spent the past few days in shock. I mean, you were both expecting a fifty-fifty chance of being chosen by Wulf. Getting his cuffs. Transporting to The Colony to raise little Wulf pups."

The crowd laughed, and I tried hard not to roll my eyes.

It was Genevieve who spoke first. "It was surprising, yes. Olivia has done my makeup since the first episode, so we've gotten to know each other a bit. It's so nice she found someone who wants her with such... intensity. I'm happy for her."

"That's it? No catty feelings?" Chet swung his gaze to Willow.

She smiled, a perfect beauty-pageant look. "Toward Olivia? It's obvious they are supposed to be together. I don't want to be with a guy, from Earth or not, who doesn't belong with me."

Chet looked a little disappointed that they weren't upset.

Genevieve nodded. "I agree. I want what they have, but with an Atlan of my own." She waggled her eyebrows and grinned, which made the audience hoot and whistle.

"Does this mean you're going to volunteer for the Brides Program?" Chet asked.

"Definitely."

"And you, Willow?"

"I'm happy for Wulf and Olivia. I'm ready to find a mate of my own. I'm definitely volunteering and asking for The Colony."

"What about you, Genevieve? You will choose an Atlan, then?" Chet prodded.

She shrugged her slim shoulders. "I think the testing will decide that for me."

Chet swung around and faced the camera. "Speaking of testing, I have discovered that someone on this stage has already been tested and been matched."

Whispers came from the crowd. Willow and Genevieve looked at each other. Out of the corner of my eye, I could see Wulf tense. Barely.

"Tell me, Warlord Wulf, about your testing match from a few years ago. We have discovered you had an Interstellar Bride, didn't you?"

More gasps and chatter surrounded us.

"I was matched, yes," Wulf stated.

Chet nodded like a bobblehead doll. "Please share. I'm sure everyone wants to know."

"A bride came from Earth for the thirty-day claiming period," Wulf explained neutrally. "During that time, she chose to return to Earth. That is all."

"You don't look like an alien who handles rejection well. If I remember, it required a tranquilizer." Chet swiveled back to the camera. "Unfortunately for you. However, it is very fortunate for us, folks, that we have a very special surprise guest with us tonight...Ruth Sanchez, Warlord Wulf's original matched mate."

Oh shit. While we'd both expected the story to possibly come up, I had never considered... this.

Chet stood and I whipped my head around to see a pretty woman with long dark hair and wicked curves come out onto the stage. She was exotic, gorgeous. Like a movie star. Clapping came from the audience as a stagehand brought a chair onto the stage and placed it between Wulf and Chet, dead center.

Wulf slipped his hand from mine and gripped the arms of his couch. Hard.

Oh shit. Ruth Sanchez, aka Wulf's ex-match, was magnificent. She made Genevieve and Willow look homely. Long black tresses curled artfully over her shoulders and down her back. Her skin was a gorgeous caramel color from her obvious Hispanic heritage. She smiled with the brilliance of a teeth whitening commercial. I had to admit, her makeup was flawless. Her outfit wasn't casual like Genevieve's and Willow's. Oh no. She had on an LBD, a little black dress, that was meant to impress. Fine, she was stunning. But what had doubt creeping in was that she wasn't bony like Wulf had said about the twenty-four contestants.

Ruth was what people called big-boned. No, not just that. She was an Amazon. Thick, sturdy. Tall. She wasn't Atlan big, but she could hold her own. Where I was also thick, I was soft, too. She had sinewy muscles that proved she could handle a beast. No wonder she'd been matched to an Atlan. She practically was one.

She wasn't looking at Wulf with neutral resignation as Genevieve and Willow were. It seemed they'd spent the two days since the grand finale coming to terms that Wulf wouldn't be either of theirs. Ruth Sanchez was eyeing Wulf like he was the largest piece of meat and she was a wild animal who hadn't eaten in a week.

Ruth Sanchez wanted Wulf. She'd had him first, and it looked like she was back for seconds.

When the audience quieted, Chet settled in. "Ruth, you were tested and matched to Warlord Wulf?"

"That's right. Hi, Wulf," she practically purred.

He offered a stiff nod in return.

"After testing, you transported immediately to Atlan, to Wulf?"

"Yes. That was where he lived at the time."

"Tell me about your days together... and nights," Chet added with a wink.

She crossed her long legs, and while I sat off to the side of her, I had to wonder if she'd flashed the camera *Basic Instinct*-style.

"Wulf is a gentleman. As everyone can see, gorgeous. He kept me quite busy," she said, then leaned toward Chet as if telling him a secret. "If you know what I mean."

I glanced at Wulf at her insinuation. He remained silent and stoic.

"I think the entire world is aware of how he keeps a woman busy," Chet countered, and everyone onstage turned to look at me. I knew the camera was even focused on my face. I could feel my cheeks heat under everyone's scrutiny, and I fought like hell to keep my face neutral. I was not going to give Chet anything I didn't have to.

"Yes, well, I'm sure Olivia's gotten him warmed up for a real woman."

"Are you that real woman?" Chet asked.

"I am all woman, as I'm sure Wulf remembers."

That bitch. I was going to claw her eyes out.

Chet laughed, then snapped his fingers. He even said, "Snap!"

Thank God he did, because I snapped out of my jealous desire to shred her face with my fingernails and noticed one of the cameras had zoomed in on my face.

Chet allowed the crowd the time to get their laughs in... at my expense. "Yet you rejected him, Ruth. Returned to Earth. Why? What happened? What went wrong? Were there problems in the bedroom?"

She sighed and glanced longingly at Wulf. "I was unused to his... virility. I didn't think I could handle all those big muscles and intense gazes. Atlans like to do it standing up, you know, especially when their beasts are in charge."

Oh brother. Chet was a sleazeball, and Ruth was playing right along. I decided to hate them both.

But then, she was right. Which meant she and Wulf...his beast?

No. No. No. Not going there. He was mine now. Not hers. Right?

Chet cleared his throat as if what she said bothered his sensibilities and he couldn't speak of such things on TV. "So you didn't really answer my question. He didn't satisfy you? Is that why you rejected him?"

"The opposite. I'd been young and innocent then. I had left a boy back home, someone I naively thought I was in love with. Wulf had been *too* much for someone so young. He was so big and so intense. I had never felt anything like that before. I think I wasn't mature enough to handle all that...passion."

She was inferring they'd had sex. Beast sex. I didn't know what to think. I had no doubt Wulf had been eager for a match and had been voracious for her when he'd first seen her. I wasn't into women, and I could see her appeal. I'd want to fuck her, too.

"So you returned to Earth and married the young boy you'd left behind. That sounds very romantic."

I glanced at her left hand. No ring.

Ruth nodded and waved her hand in the air. "It was a huge mistake. Letting Wulf go was the biggest mistake of my life. I realized that what I'd been so afraid of with Wulf was what I wanted. What my body needed. My husband and I divorced after three months."

"So you're available and eager for a beast to tame you."

A slow smile spread across her face as she looked Wulf over. "Yes. I meet all the Brides Program criteria. I was matched to Atlan and then to Wulf. If I walked into a bride testing center again, I have no doubt we'd be matched again. We are perfect for each other."

"What are you saying, Ruth? That Wulf and Olivia are not right for each other? That you want him back? That you are still in love with him?"

The audience was dead quiet. It didn't take a rocket scientist to know what was coming. So did Chet, because he created a very long, pregnant pause.

I was waiting... waiting...

Ruth took a deep breath and stared straight into the

camera. "I'm ready for my second chance with Warlord Wulf. Those cuffs are mine."

The audience went crazy.

"We'll see if she gets them after these messages." Chet had to stand and practically yell to be heard over the audience.

Wulf immediately turned his body to face me and opened his mouth to speak.

"Okay! Time to clear the stage," the producer shouted, jumping up onto the dais and waving his arms. "Only Chet with Wulf and Ruth after the commercial."

I frowned as he came over to me. "Come on, doll. We only have a minute before the break is over. Go with Genevieve and Willow to watch backstage."

He reached for my arm to lift me from the chair, but Wulf growled and the producer stepped back. Clearly he remembered what happened the last time Wulf growled.

I looked to Wulf, then Ruth.

She wasn't afraid. She looked thrilled. I looked to Wulf, whose gaze was focused on me. Was that rage in his eyes? Guilt? She was perfect, his perfect match. She was curvy and gorgeous and wanted him. Shit. I would not cry. Would *not*.

"Olivia—" Wulf reached for me, but I held up a hand to keep him in his seat.

"It's okay. I'm okay."

He settled in the chair. "I must finish this, for the others on The Colony."

I nodded. "I know. It's all right. I'm fine." Genevieve stopped beside me, and I stood, then walked offstage with her and Willow.

The three of us stood in the darkness behind the cameras to watch. Wulf stared in my direction, but I knew from being up there with the lights shining in your eyes, it was impossible to see anything offstage. Ruth moved her chair closer to Wulf, and she leaned into him, the bounty of her cleavage right there for Wulf—and all of Earth—to see.

The cameraman indicated the countdown.

"Welcome back!" Chet crooned. "We're here with Warlord Wulf, who, as you know, chose a makeup artist from our staff as his mate in a surprising and wild way the other night." He stood, went over to the display case where the cuffs were showcased. "Yet here are the cuffs. They are not on Olivia Mercier's wrists. After the beast's appearance the other night, I expected Wulf to rip the glass off and get those cuffs on his mate at the very beginning of this show. What a fairy tale that would have been. It makes me wonder if that was ever his intention. Who said flings were only for humans?"

He'd called me a fling. On national—no, on international television. Oh. My. God.

I wrung my hands together, felt my bare wrists. He hadn't put them on me. He'd been so desperate to do so. It was one of the reasons for our being here today. Yet they were still behind that glass.

I knew Wulf held it together so he could represent the fighters on The Colony favorably. He didn't want to scare women away from the Brides Program a second time, but still... he held back. He wasn't saying a word.

"Looks like we have a catfight on our hands and the cuffs are up for grabs," Chet murmured and moved to his seat once again. "With me, onstage, is Ruth Sanchez, Warlord Wulf's matched mate from the Interstellar Brides Program. They were matched four years ago, and she regrets her decision to return to Earth. Now she's back for a second chance. Isn't that right, Ruth?"

Ruth nodded, her glossy hair sliding over her shoulders. "Yes, Chet. I was wrong. Seeing Wulf these past few weeks with the contestants on the show allowed me to see a different side of him."

"How so?" Chet wondered.

"Well, when I knew him, he hadn't been captured by the Hive. Tortured. Integrated." She reached out, grabbed Wulf's hand and hugged it to her bountiful breasts.

"Oh, she didn't," Willow whispered.

Yeah, she totally did.

"My mate is so much calmer now. Mature."

"What about the beast that tore up the stage the other night?" Chet wondered. "That was far from calm."

"It wasn't the little makeup artist he scented, Chet. I was..." She looked away as if ashamed, then back at the camera. "I was in the audience. He had to have scented me. That's why he went crazy, because he couldn't find me."

Wulf's knuckles went white as he gripped the chair, but he remained still. Quiet.

"Wow, she's ruthless," Genevieve whispered.

Willow nodded.

Yeah, she was. I couldn't look at them, just stared at Wulf, who remained almost... stony. Why wasn't he refuting her words? I had no doubt that audiences around the world were gobbling this up as the tastiest fodder.

Had he really slept with her and been too much? I'd seen the dominant, beast side of him, but the more tender lover as well.

"He grabbed Olivia Mercier and took her to one of the back rooms. They... ahem, became acquainted."

"I've been *acquainted* with Wulf, too." She offered a small shrug as if she didn't give a shit. "She's not wearing the cuffs."

Yeah, she didn't give a shit at all. She wanted Wulf back.

Chet didn't respond, only looked to Wulf.

When neither guy did anything, Ruth stood, slid her snug dress up her thighs a few inches, climbed onto Wulf's lap, then kissed him.

Willow gasped.

Genevieve took her hand in mine. She leaned close, whispered, "He wants you."

I stared at Ruth's body practically glued to Wulf's. Her hands cupped his face as she kissed him like she had a beast inside her.

I couldn't see his face, but Wulf's hand moved to her lower back.

I felt sick at the sight. He was engaging, not pushing her away. Had he been in love with her? He'd said he'd been upset at her rejection, but had he changed his mind now that he'd had a second taste? Was he still in love with her?

Ruth lifted her head, and I could see she had lust—and triumph—on her face.

Wulf turned her so she sat on his lap and he could see Chet.

"Get the cuffs from the case for me?" Wulf asked him.

Chet popped up faster than toast in a toaster.

"I can't watch," I whispered. Genevieve took my hand and led me off the set. I was thankful for her help because I wasn't paying any attention to where I was going. Once we were out in a hall where we could talk, she turned me to face her.

"Are you okay?"

I swallowed back tears. "No."

"I can't believe it. He's going to give the cuffs to her? Now? In front of everyone?"

"I don't know. Looks like it."

"Do you really think he smelled her in the audience the other night?"

Was that possible? I knew how he'd been in that back room. Wild and frantic for me. Yet had it been Ruth's scent that made him wild and I'd somehow gotten in his path? Whatever had happened was irrelevant. It seemed everything that had happened in the past two days was, too. He'd requested the cuffs, and Ruth was pretty much humping his leg like a bitch in heat.

That was mean, but I couldn't take it back, not even in my own mind.

"I have to get out of here." I turned and ran blindly down the hallway. I heard Genevieve running behind me. I didn't stop until I was out on the sidewalk, New Yorkers all around me.

"I'll get you a cab." Genevieve lifted her fingers to her mouth with one hand and let out an earsplitting whistle while flagging down a passing taxi with the other. It pulled up in front of me.

"Thanks, Genevieve," I said as she hugged me tight.

"Don't worry, we'll all get the guys of our dreams."

When I climbed in the cab and told the driver the name of the hotel, I sat back and wondered if I ever would.

12

W ulf

CONTROL THE BEAST. *Control the beast.* CONTROL THE BEAST!

I was doing everything in my power to keep my beast from tossing Ruth Sanchez across the set. I didn't hurt women and I never tossed one, but the need to do so was almost impossible to resist. Yet I maintained control. Barely.

I'd destroyed one set already. Destroying this one would only prove that deserving fighters from other planets couldn't be controlled or trusted with Earth females. I owed it to the Atlan warlords who had suffered as I had, Braun and Tane, Kai and Egon and all the fighters from the planets banished to The Colony, to hold myself in check. I was doing this for them. All of this. Every torturous second of my time on this planet.

Except when I was with Olivia. And that didn't include now. Chet had herded her from the stage along with

Genevieve and Willow, as if they were discarded weapons no longer loaded with ammunition. He'd used them for what he wanted and was finished with them.

I knew they stood just beyond the cameras, as Olivia had the other night when I'd discovered her. My mate wasn't alone, but with the two finalists. I didn't like her out of my sight, but I had no option at this moment. Chet knew what he was doing. So did the producer. They were taunting me. The beast inside. They wanted this to go on... and on.

They wanted another spectacle. They wanted me to lose control.

I would not give in. So instead of tossing, I stood abruptly, Ruth Sanchez sliding down my body and landing on the raised platform in an undignified heap. She gasped and the audience laughed. While I wished to shame her, as she had blatantly lied and was misusing me for her own fame and gain, I couldn't dishonor her in such a way. I took her hand and hoisted her to her feet, quickly moving her so she stood several feet away.

During this time, Chet had done as I'd asked and retrieved the cuffs from the glass case. They were my other goal. I would have them in my hands where no one dared take them from me. If he collected them under the assumption I was giving them to Ruth Sanchez, then so be it. If the audience believed I'd scorned Olivia for the lying female who'd long ago rejected me for another, so be it.

They would learn the truth soon enough.

Chet held the cuffs out in front of him. Two sets, one large for my wrists, one small for my mate's. "Aren't they beautiful, folks? Prettier than a diamond solitaire." He winked at the camera. "Especially if they come with an Altan like Warlord Wulf."

Gritting my teeth, I held myself still instead of stalking over to him and ripping them from his fingers.

"It appears a change of heart has occurred." Some audience members clapped, others booed. "Now, now. Even Atlans can be fickle when it comes to love. I mean, when you have to choose between a duckling like Olivia Mercier and a swan such as Ruth Sanchez..."

My beast rumbled at the blatant insult to my mate. I didn't know much about Earth animals, but I understood his meaning well enough. Chet glanced my way and blanched, clearly realizing he may have gone too far.

"Who will he choose? We'll find out after these messages," Chet said quickly, and the camera light went out.

I'd had enough, and I could move and speak freely now that there was a break. I took the two Atlan-sized steps between me and Chet and plucked the cuffs from his fingers. The cool metal felt good in my hands. Reaching back, I clipped my cuffs on the back of my belt and held on to the smaller ones.

"Where is Olivia?" I asked, looking out into the darkness off set.

"You can put them on me now, Wulf. I'm ready," Ruth said, but I ignored her.

"Olivia, come here."

She didn't appear. I waited.

"Olivia?" I called again.

Stepping from the darkness wasn't my mate, but Willow. "She's gone, Wulf."

My beast howled and pushed right at the surface. I had to stay calm. I couldn't lose it. Not this time. Not here. If I had to leave the building to find her, I couldn't be in beast form. I'd be shot. Or on the news. Or both. I owed it to my friends on The Colony to give them a chance. But I had to find my mate. Now.

"Where did she go?" I asked, stepping down from the platform.

Willow wasn't afraid of me, thankfully, because she came to stand right in front of me. "You had your hand on Ruth's ass. The woman was kissing you. You asked for the cuffs."

"Yes, I asked for them so I could give them to Olivia."

Her mouth dropped open. "Really? Because it looked like you were going to give them to Ruth."

I shook my head. "I don't want Ruth. I know now I never did. It was the only way to get Chet to take them from the case."

She smiled. "That was smart."

I shook my head. "I want Olivia. Where. Is. She?"

Her smile fell away. "I don't know. She couldn't stay and watch you give the cuffs to another woman. You hurt her."

Fuck. How had this show ruined everything? No. Not everything. Without it I never would have met Olivia.

I spun on my heel and faced Chet Bosworth and Ruth Sanchez. "The cuffs are for Olivia Mercier, my mate. Ruth, never. Chet, I'm done. End the show with that. If I hear you cutting down the other fighters on The Colony, I will be back, and I will crush more than your audio amplifier."

I cut through the backstage area.

"I'll help you." I slowed at Willow's rushed words, knew she was running to keep up. I looked down into her pretty face.

"Olivia would have gone to the hotel to get the children."

She frowned at that but said nothing. "Do you know the name of the hotel?"

I nodded.

"We'll get you a taxi. Come on." She led the way down a flight of stairs and outside. She waved at a yellow vehicle, which didn't stop. She waved at another, which also didn't stop for her. I caught on to what she was doing, and when I saw a third yellow vehicle coming our way, I stepped onto the street and held up my arms. The yellow vehicle stopped.

"Here, you'll need this." She stuffed small pieces of paper in my hands. "It's money for the cab. Good luck, Wulf. Maybe I'll see you on The Colony someday soon."

I took her arm and moved her away from the front of the vehicle. "Thank you, Willow. I do as well. You will make a fine mate for a worthy warrior."

"Thank you, Wulf." Her smile was a bit shy, and I realized that I truly did hope both she and Genevieve claimed worthy males. They were smart, beautiful women, but not the one I wanted.

Climbing into the back was almost impossible, but I wedged myself in and told the driver where I wanted to go. He took off, thankfully, like a fighter ship from deep space. Hopefully I wasn't too late. Olivia was mine, although at this moment, she might not believe it.

I had to fix that, and then I could take my family home.

13

Why was I so upset? I'd been telling myself this was going to happen since we met. I'd told him he was mistaken from the very beginning, practically the very first words I ever said to him. I *knew* something was going to go wrong. Knew it.

Wulf was too good to be true. Too... everything. I was not his type. Gorgeous warrior gods did *not* go for women like me. Maybe for a fling, to empty their balls, but as something real?

No. They went with women like *her*. Ruth. While she wasn't model small, she was exactly the big Amazon woman Wulf needed. This also included expensive perfume, designer clothes, lip injections, expensive spike heels and breast implants. In other words, gorgeous.

The only thing real about that woman had been the triumph in her eyes after she'd climbed up in Wulf's lap and kissed him. She couldn't have been any more obvious, and the cameras ate it up. On top of that, Wulf had asked for the cuffs. Supposedly my cuffs. Chet had retrieved them so Wulf could put them on *her*. His real mate. His *perfect match* from the Interstellar Brides Program. His true mate. The perfect woman for him.

I couldn't compete with not only the perfect female specimen but the actual bride test. It had chosen *her* for *him*. The test didn't lie. Wulf deserved to be with the perfect woman. After what he'd survived? Not some overweight makeup artist who had inherited two kids from a deadbeat brother and struggled to pay the mortgage every month.

The taxi pulled to a stop in front of the hotel, and I handed him my money in silence, not trusting my voice. The doorman opened the door of the car, and I ducked my head, practically running past him as the tears welled up. I would *not* cry in the hotel lobby. Would not. I had some dignity left. Some pride. I was *not* broken.

I had survived worse than Warlord Wulf of Atlan. That was for damn sure. It was amazing how much I hurt over a guy I'd only known for two days. Two days and I was a complete wreck!

The elevator was a welcome reprieve from too curious eyes, and I leaned back, letting my head hit the hard, cool surface on the way up to the twenty-first floor. Lucy would be there, with that knowing look in her eyes. Hopefully she'd turned the television off when things went sideways. If Tanner and Emma had seen Wulf kiss that horrible woman... Well, I didn't know what I would do about that or what Wulf did when he'd found me gone. No, he wouldn't go all beast again because his mate had been straddling his lap and sucking the tonsils from his throat.

The ride was over too soon—thankfully no one had

gotten on—and I stood before my hotel room door, the *Do Not Disturb* sign clearly displayed. I expected to hear the sounds of Tanner and Emma even out here in the hallway. Instead an odd quiet made my skin chill.

Unlocking the door with the key card I'd gotten from the front desk, I walked in to find the room silent and dark, the blackout curtains completely closed. The television was off. The lights were off. The room was empty.

What the hell?

I flipped on the switch, and one sad little side lamp lit up next to the bed. "Lucy?"

Alarmed now, I hurried to find another light switch and flipped it on. The bed was a mess where the kids had probably played. The connecting door to the suite I shared with Wulf was closed. Maybe they were in the other room?

I walked toward the door but stopped dead in my tracks at the sight of two feet sticking out of the bathroom door. Lucy's favorite slipper socks, a pair of fuzzy panda faces staring up at me from the floor. I blinked, then gasped, my brain finally catching up to my eyes.

"Lucy?" Shock slowed my movements as I stepped into the open doorframe to see Lucy bound, gagged and unconscious, lying on the bathroom floor. "Oh my God! Lucy!"

Kneeling beside her, I tore at the duct tape that circled her wrists, but I'd need a knife to cut through. My movements stirred her, and she tried to speak. I pulled the tape from her mouth, and she worked to spit one of Tanner's dinosaur socks out. I yanked the green and yellow sock free.

"What happened? Are you all right? Where are Tanner and Emma? Where are they?"

Her green eyes were blurry, and she winced, clearly not one hundred percent. "You tell me. Who is Jimmy Steel?"

I felt the blood drain from my face, and I dropped down onto the cold tile, trying once again to get her hands free. "No. Impossible."

Lucy moaned in pain as she tried to sit up, and I hurried to help her. "Call the cops," she slurred. "He took them. He took Tanner and Emma."

My hands, which had been tearing at the duct tape around her wrists, froze. "What? What did you say?"

Tears welled in her eyes, and she lifted her bound hands to the back of her head. "He took them, Liv. He took them. He left you a box."

Panic filled me. Hot. Intense. Frantic. Tanner and Emma weren't here. They weren't safe. I had no idea where they were, but I did know they were with a very bad man. Hurting innocent children would be something he'd do and not think twice.

No!

Shit. Shit. Shit. This was not happening. I yanked at the heavy silver tape around her ankles as she twisted her wrists free. "God. No. This is wrong. This isn't happening."

"Who is Jimmy Steel?" she repeated.

It wasn't like I could keep this secret from her any longer. She'd been hurt by him. Bound and gagged. "He's... he's a guy Greg owed money. When he died, Jimmy came to me and made me take over the debt. Those errands I ran were drug runs."

"Oh my God, Liv," she said, eyes wide with panic. "Where's Wulf? Turn him loose on this Jimmy guy. He'll rip him and his asshole goons in half. Literally."

I shook my head. "Wulf is out of the picture."

She stared at me with wide eyes. "What?"

"You didn't see the show?"

155

She huffed. "I was a little busy with some bad guys, and then I was on the bathroom floor. Not much opportunity."

I pursed my lips. While I knew her words were laced with heavy sarcasm, I felt guilty for getting her into this mess. I couldn't imagine how she'd felt when the kids were taken from her.

I pulled Lucy carefully to her feet, then had to wrap my arm around her waist as she swayed, unstable. I helped her to the main room and settled her in a chair, and I sank to my knees in front of her, holding her hands.

"Call the cops. Do it. Then tell me what happened to Wulf because we could sure use him right now."

I got up and paced. I couldn't call the cops. Jimmy had been very clear in his threats to me. First he'd hurt Tanner and Emma. Then Lucy. Then my seventy-seven-year-old grandmother in an assisted living facility. She might not remember me, but she was still family. My cousins. We never spoke, their dubious life choices not meshing with mine, but they were blood. My blood. Greg's blood. They didn't deserve to be hurt or killed by Jimmy Steel.

Thanks to my dead brother and his big mouth, Jimmy had a ready-made list of every living, breathing person on the planet that I cared about. At all. Every. Single. One.

Fuck.

Shaking my head, I met her pain-filled eyes. "I can't call the cops."

"Why not?" Lucy was rubbing her temples like she had a bitch of a headache. She probably did.

"Do you need to go to the hospital?"

"No. I'll be fine. Where's Wulf?"

"Ruth Sanchez," I muttered. "That's what happened. His perfect matched mate showed up. He had a bride, apparently. An Interstellar Bride who didn't stay with him when they were first matched a few years ago. She showed up, said she made a mistake, that she wants him back. She sat in his lap and kissed him on live TV, Luce. He had his hands all over her, and then he asked Chet to give him his cuffs."

"Oh, sweetie. No."

"He didn't even look at me. So I left. I couldn't watch him put them on her wrists. I couldn't do it."

"I'm so sorry. You fell in love with him, didn't you?"

I couldn't speak, so I nodded. As dumb as it was, I had fallen for him. Hard. "I don't care about Wulf right now. I need to find the kids."

She wobbled, but she stood and came to wrap me in a hug. We were both shaken up, and we clung to each other like frightened children. "What are we going to do? I knew something was wrong every time you asked me to babysit. You should have told me about this Jimmy guy."

I sighed. "He was Greg's loan shark who dabbles in all kinds of stuff. Drugs, prostitution and more," I repeated. "When Greg died, he owed Jimmy a lot of money. He came to me to collect, threatened Tanner and Emma"—*and you*, I thought, but I didn't say it out loud—"if I didn't cooperate. We made a deal. I did a few drops for him 'cause I look more like a soccer mom than a drug mule, paid him some cash and returned all the money owed. The other night, when you watched the kids?"

"Yeah?"

"That was my last drop. I left the show, made the drop, came home. It was supposed to be over. I kept my end of the deal. I did what he wanted."

She shook her head but winced. "It's never enough, not for guys like that. Not when they know they can use you over and over. The kids are leverage."

I sank onto the couch. "Now he has Tanner and Emma. If I call the cops, he'll hurt them. I know him, Lucy. He'll hurt them." I broke down then, the tears streaming down my cheeks as I fought to hold in the out-of-control, racking sobs I knew were right behind them if I didn't at least try to hold myself together.

"Then we take him down."

I looked up at her determined face. "How?"

"I don't know."

I popped back up, paced. "I need a gun. Where can I buy a gun in New York?"

"That's crazy talk."

"Is it?" I wiped my cheeks and took a deep breath. I would cry later, when it was over. I'd think about Wulf and Ruth and what a mess my life was later. Right now I had to get Tanner and Emma home safe. That was the only thing that mattered. "What did Jimmy say? What does he want?"

Lucy pointed and dread made my heart heavy as I approached the table nearest the window. Sitting in the center was a rather large box, black, tied with a pretty bow.

Hand shaking, I untied the black satin bow from the box and lifted the lid.

"What is it?" Lucy asked.

"I don't know." A cream-colored envelope lay atop a layer of black tissue paper, my name written in a scrawl I recognized all too well. Jimmy Steel's handwriting.

The envelope was not sealed, and the paper felt like soft fabric as I pulled out a single card, finer than anything I'd ever touched before. The invitation was handwritten, in ink, the calligraphy elegantly curved and beautiful. Ironic that something so beautiful felt like holding death in my hands.

I read aloud. "Your presence is requested at the New York Gala Event for the I-I-M-A-A. The International,

Interplanetary and Multicultural Arts Alliance." I glanced at the clock on the bedside table. "Oh God. It started fifteen minutes ago."

I didn't read Jimmy's handwritten note aloud. Lucy had been through enough.

Embarrass me and Emma dies first.

Embarrass him? What if I wasn't there, what was Jimmy going to do to the kids? To Lucy the next time his goons got his hands on her? To everyone I knew? This was a nightmare, and I missed Wulf so much I felt like a barbed dagger was being shoved—one agonizing bit at a time— right into my heart. I turned away from Lucy so she wouldn't see me clutching at my chest. That was all I needed right now, a heart attack.

"I have never even heard of this Arts Alliance. Why does he want you to go?" Lucy was rubbing her temple now, and I was grateful she remained in the chair with her head down so she wouldn't see me shaking. "That doesn't even make sense."

"No, it doesn't." I placed the invitation on the side table and pulled back the tissue paper. "Holy shit."

livia

THE TAXI RIDE WAS UNEVENTFUL. The gown I wore was more befitting a beauty queen than me, but somehow Jimmy Steel had included everything I needed to pull this off, in all the right sizes.

That meant he was either an amazing talent in women's clothing—which I doubted—or he'd had someone watching me for months. Stalking me. Taking fucking notes. I had to choke down the bile rising in the back of my throat at the thought.

But I had on lingerie that was softer than my own skin. The dress fit like a glove, highlighting all the right curves and hugging the rest tight. Even the shoes were spectacular and fit me perfectly.

Lucy had worked a five-minute miracle with my makeup. I had no idea what I was walking into, but I did know two things. One, I didn't have a gun. Even if I'd wanted to get one, I didn't have time or anywhere to hide it in this dress. And two, Wulf wasn't coming to help, to rip their heads off as Lucy wanted. I'd made sure of that.

In fact, I'd called the producer and left him a voice message to congratulate Wulf on his happy reunion with Ruth—*I would hate her forever for stealing my man*—Sanchez, his *perfect* match. I figured that would wrap up the show as he wanted, get the sound bite needed so I'd get some kind of job in the future. I'd hung up and cried for all of two minutes before Lucy reminded me that the kids needed me. Tanner and Emma. I had to focus on them. I'd claw Jimmy's eyes out with my fingernails if I had to, to make sure he never threatened them again.

As a bellman opened the taxi's door, I paid the driver and allowed the tuxedo-clad gentleman on the curb to assist me to the door. I should be completely focused on Jimmy, on this event, on what the hell was happening right now. But no.

Instead, every time I blinked, I saw Ruth's lips on Wulf's, his hand on her ass as she straddled him, heard the gasps from the audience and saw Chet—*Drama King*—Bosworth's satisfied smile, and I wanted to crumble into flakes like month-old bread crust. That wouldn't do. I had to hold myself together. For Emma and Tanner.

"Your invitation, miss." The bellman handed me off to what had to be a bouncer, also in a tuxedo, who was checking invitations and keeping out people who shouldn't be here. People like me. I had no business being in this marble-columned event center. The building was intimidating, looked like a courthouse... or a castle.

Forcing a smile, I handed him the linen paper and

waited until he gave a slight nod to yet another person on the inside of a glass door. The door opened, and a woman in an elegant white satin gown walked forward to greet me.

"Welcome. Welcome. You look stunning, dear. Truly beautiful."

"Thank you." Was that her job? To give every person who walked in overstated compliments?

"What is your name?" she asked. "I will escort you to your table for the evening."

When I offered it, she nodded, not needing to check any list that I could see. "Of course. If you would follow me."

She led the way toward the front of a grand ballroom set with round tables the likes of which I had never seen. Flowers cascaded from every wall. The tables were set with dishes for dinner, the fine china so thin I could see through the coffee cups as I walked past, all of it decorated with gold filigree I did not doubt was real. The crystal looked expensive; the people looked like they were from another planet. Literally. I had never seen so much gold or jewelry. The diamonds in this room could probably fund a small nation's economy for years.

Not one person glanced my way for the first half of my journey. Then I heard the first gasp, a woman's voice, of course. Followed by, "Isn't that the woman from that *Bachelor Beast* show?"

"Oh my God, I think it is."

Then a few more murmurs. By the time my guide and I reached the table I assumed was our destination, I had attracted a small crowd and was not paying attention to anyone seated there waiting for me. Until I heard *his* voice.

"Ah, there you are, my lovely. What took you so long?" Jimmy Steel stood to greet me, an empty seat beside him, the *only* empty seat at the table. He looked handsome, civilized in a black suit and tie, yet I knew the monster that lurked beneath the facade. His scowl drove off the curious who had been following me, and surely they sensed what I did. He was a demon in the flesh.

Embarrass me and Emma dies first.

I couldn't make a scene, and there were at least two women who had taken out their phones—discreetly, of course—who were, without doubt, recording every moment. I realized a photographer was slowly making his way from the opposite side of the room as well. His camera pointed in our direction. Most likely he had one of those long-range lenses and had already taken pictures. Shit. This was not what I was expecting. Not at all. Before, it had all been in secret. Now? Everyone knew I was *with* Jimmy Steel.

"What do you want, Jimmy?" I looked around the room, then returned my gaze to where he stood, waiting for me to sit. Like a gentleman, he'd pulled out my chair.

"My dear, I simply want you to meet some friends." His gaze raked over me, and he took his sweet time about it, making me even more uncomfortable. "You look amazing in that dress. We'll go for a drink later."

Was that an invitation or a threat? He couldn't be serious. My level of interest in *any* relationship since I'd mistakenly believed I'd found the love of my life with an alien Atlan warlord named Wulf was a big, fat zero. With Jimmy? Well, when hell froze over wasn't long enough. No. Hell would have to freeze, thaw out, burn for a while and then freeze again. Oh, and then I'd have to be dead before I would willingly spend time with the man.

I didn't respond to his invitation or say thank you for the compliment despite the audience. I could not get the words past my lips.

Embarrass me and Emma dies first.

"Where are Tanner and Emma?"

"They are here, of course. With the other children." He waved a hand, and I noticed a large section of one wall was made of glass. Behind it, a number of well-dressed children ran and played. In the middle of the group, laughing and looking like they didn't have a care in the world, were my niece and nephew. Safe.

Thank God. My knees buckled for the briefest of seconds, and it was Jimmy's hand that came to my elbow to steady me. His touch made my skin crawl.

"What do you want, Jimmy?" I repeated the question, because if he'd given me an answer, my addled brain had missed it completely.

"I saw what happened earlier on TV, with that Ruth woman, was it? I thought you might enjoy a night out to forget about it." He used the hand on my elbow to his advantage and led me to the chair reserved for me with a handwritten card.

Miss Olivia Mercier. Like I belonged here. What a joke.

Jimmy sat next to me and smiled, a huge, show-every-tooth-in-his-mouth smile, his voice loud and directed at the other occupants of the table. "Olivia, my lovely. I knew you would appreciate a night out, and my closest friends wanted to meet you."

If Jimmy had one true friend, I was a brain surgeon. But whatever. The kids were safe. They were in a public place. The chair that I sat in, right next to Jimmy, was strategically placed so I could keep the kids in view. Smart. Jimmy Steel was one of the smartest criminals on the planet.

The table held two other couples, all in their sixties if they were a day. Each one of them wore more money in clothes, jewelry and shoes than I made in a year.

"James, dear, introduce us to your beautiful date."

Date? I was not his fucking date. I was his hostage. And *James*? No one called him that. No one I knew, and I knew just about every top-level drug distributor he ruled over in Miami.

His hand clamped down on mine on top of the table, and I held my tongue, forced a smile.

"I'd like you all to meet the lovely Olivia Mercier." He nodded and tilted his chin as if he were the best boyfriend on the planet. "Olivia, this is Marcia and Walter Smith, and Agnes and Harold Jenaway."

The second name rang a bell. I'd heard it somewhere before. I looked more closely.

"Senator Jenaway? From Florida?"

She chuckled and her beaming husband took her hand in the same way Jimmy's still covered mine. I doubted Harold had to squeeze quite so hard to keep his wife from breaking free. "My dear, I told you someone would recognize you here."

She smiled back at him, their banter natural and easy, as if they'd been married forever and could read each other's thoughts. "You were right, Harold. As usual. New York is not that far from Florida."

He lifted their joined hands to his mouth and kissed her knuckles. "What would you do without me?" he asked.

She leaned in and kissed him on the cheek. "You know, dearest, I really loved that silver and stone sculpture from Prillon Prime. Do you think you could go check the bids again?"

"Of course." He winked at me as he rose. "Happy wife, happy life. Right, Olivia?"

I nodded mutely as the other couple, Marcia and Walter,

rose, as if on cue, the wife speaking in an apologetic whisper.

"I have my eye on the platinum cuffs from Atlan." She glanced around as if afraid someone might overhear her. "I really, really want them, and I don't want anyone to outbid me."

Her husband had his hand at the small of her back as he led her away. "No one is going to outbid you, dear. You already offered a small fortune."

"You never know."

"Yes, dear."

The trio wandered off to what I assumed was some kind of alien art display area, which left me with Jimmy—who finally let go of my hand, thank God—and Senator Agnes Jenaway, from Miami, who suddenly looked less than friendly.

"I'm glad you accepted our invitation, Olivia," she said.

"Our invitation?" Her choice of words had me clearing my throat. "Is that what you call it?"

She smiled and sipped from her crystal goblet filled with white wine. "Of course. The children look lovely, don't you agree? Happy? Well-groomed? Without a care in the world?" She looked over to where they played, a satisfied gleam in her gaze. "I chose their outfits myself. What handsome children. You take good care of them, dear."

What was she getting at? What did she want? "I do my best."

"Of course you do. That's a mother's job. Isn't it, James?"

"Yes, Mother."

Mother? What? *WHAT*?

"Close your mouth, dear girl. Didn't your mother teach you any manners?" The senator scolded me, and I closed my mouth like an obedient child.

"What do you want?" I asked again. Jimmy Steel was James Jenaway? Son of a senator? What the hell?

"What do you think I want?" she asked.

I was going to kill her. Jimmy. Everyone in this damn room. The waiter leaned forward to fill her glass with more wine, and she waived him off with a soft thank-you and a request for a few moments of privacy.

"Yes ma'am." The innocent server walked to stand along the wall where she could summon his return with one crook of her twisted, evil finger.

"Now that we're alone, Olivia, James and I have a proposition for you."

"What kind of proposition?" Every other moment my gaze drifted to where Emma and Tanner played, oblivious to the danger. The threat to them.

"First, I must ask, did you truly fall in love with that alien? What was his name? Warlord Wulf?"

"I don't know what that has to do with anything."

My nonanswer was, apparently, all the answer she needed, because she smiled and my stomach dropped. "Of course you did. So handsome, so virile, so different from all the human men who perhaps didn't appreciate your... Rubenesque figure."

Was she calling me fat now? "What. Do. You. Want?"

"The question, dear, is what do *you* want?"

When I remained silent, she continued.

"You see, this woman, Ruth Sanchez, is as much a problem for me and my plans as she is for you. I have asked James to make arrangements for her, so that she will no longer stand in my way. Or yours."

"I don't understand."

"Yes, you do. Don't play dumb with me. She ruined your chances with the alien you love. She ruined my plans for a very successful business alliance with a brand-new, world-famous, human bride on The Colony. Ruth will conveniently disappear, and our plans will resume. Yours and mine, my dear. You will have Wulf back, crawling on his knees, and I will have you exactly where I want you."

I had a horrible idea where this was going. "Where is that?"

"The Colony, of course. With your children, living the life of your dreams. Win-win."

Jimmy sat next to me in silence, content to allow his mother to shine in her role as evil mastermind. "He doesn't want me," I insisted. "He is in love with Ruth."

"True. You will be his second choice, but does it really matter, if you get him in the end?"

Yes, it mattered. "What good would I do you on The Colony? I don't understand what you want from me."

"You will be a bride. Trusted. Adored. You will have access to everything. Weapons. Technology. Art. There is an art dealer on Viken, a human bride named Sophia Antonelli. She helped organize this event tonight, all the way from Viken. You will be able to contact her at your whim. I want it all, and you are going to get it for me. I will give you twenty percent of the take and my personal guarantee that no one you care about will meet with any unexpected accidents once you leave Earth behind."

Sure, I wanted Wulf, but he wanted Ruth, and I wanted him to be happy. He deserved to be happy. I wasn't a murderer. No matter how much I envied Ruth Sanchez right now, I couldn't agree to this. But what was I going to do? Jimmy had already threatened Lucy. My cousins? I didn't spend time with them, but I didn't want them killed either. My grandmother?

There had to be a way out. Alaska, maybe? South America? Somewhere I could take Tanner and Emma and disappear, somewhere out of a freaking senator's reach? Where, exactly, was that? Mars?

There were rumors she was going to run for vice president in a few years. She was rich. Powerful. Connected. God help me, she probably had assassins on speed dial—on both sides of the law.

"What if I don't agree to this?" I asked.

"Then you are the one who disappears." Jimmy kissed my cheek after he whispered the words, his breath reeking of cigar smoke and gin.

"Tanner and Emma?" I asked.

She sipped her wine and waved the waiter back over. "I'm sure I know a judge who can make sure they are placed with the right foster family once you are... not here to care for them."

Jimmy's grin was lecherous, and I did not mistake her meaning. She'd make sure they ended up somewhere terrible. Truly terrible with no one to protect them.

I was going to throw up. Right now. All over this beautiful gown in front of all these people. This was not dropping off drugs at some seedy bar. This was worse. So much worse. But I needed Wulf to be happy. He had to be. I couldn't sacrifice Ruth's life and Wulf's happiness because my brother had been an asshole. This was my problem. I would deal with it alone. Like I did everything else in my life.

"I'll volunteer, okay? I will go to the Interstellar Brides Processing Center and I'll volunteer. I'll request The Colony. Just don't do anything to Ruth. Or to me." I held the older woman's gaze and made sure the hatred I felt shined through free and clear. "Do not touch my children. Do you understand me?"

"Of course. I'm not a monster." She sounded so... rational.

Jimmy leaned back in his chair and finished off the last finger of gin. "See, Mother? I told you she'd be reasonable."

"Yes, ma'am. What can I get you?" the waiter asked a smiling Agnes Jenaway.

"Pour Olivia a drink, would you? She needs it."

The waiter came around the table and filled my crystal goblet. With a shaky hand I sipped the wine as my mind whirled. I had bought some time but not much. If they did any research at all, they would realize I could not volunteer and take two small children with me. I'd already tried that. The only reason I would have been able to go with Wulf, bringing Tanner and Emma, was because I would have already been his mate. I had to get out of New York and disappear. Like, really disappear. New name. New place. New everything.

Harold, Marcia and Walter returned to the table as the waiter placed an appetizer plate in front of me. Without missing a beat, Agnes turned to her husband and raised her cheek for a kiss—as if she hadn't threatened to kill me and torture my children. "Well? How do the bids look for the piece from Prillon Prime?"

Harold grinned. "No one has outbid you yet."

She lifted her glass to her lips and sipped, watching me over the rim. "They won't."

Walter held out his chair for his wife, then sat, rubbing his hands together. "Time to eat! Dinner should be excellent. I heard they flew in a chef from Italy."

"Everyone has a price." Harold placed his napkin on his

lap as the waiter set his appetizer plate in front of him. He glanced up with a smile for me. "Hungry, Olivia?"

Agnes lifted her brows and waited for my answer. Obediently I lifted my fork. "Of course."

She smiled, and I lifted the fork to my lips, tasted ashes in my mouth. I was sipping more wine, washing down my third bite, when all hell broke loose.

15

livia

"OLIVIA!" There was no mistaking that deep voice, that roar. Wulf.

A heavy pounding sounded from the entrance, and I realized, as what looked like an entire battalion of Atlan warlords stomped into the room wearing space armor and really big space guns on their thighs, that Wulf was here. He was really here, and he wasn't alone.

As if he could scent me—which I knew he could—he beelined straight for our table and loomed over us like the giant he was.

"Jimmy Steel, I am here to claim the rights of a mate. I have come to kill you."

Men and women either scrambled to get out of the way or sat, paralyzed in their chairs, as a dozen fully armed aliens fanned out inside the ballroom. I stood, but that fast Jimmy's arm snaked around my waist and yanked me to my feet. I felt the cold press of a pistol at my temple. "One more step, Wulf, and I blow her head off."

"Injure her, and I will make you beg for death before I kill you," Wulf snarled.

Jimmy was the one shaking now, the cold steel bouncing against my cheekbone as he fought for control. I looked at Wulf, shocked that he'd come, grateful that he had.

"The children!" I shouted and pointed to the room behind glass. Two of Wulf's giant companions moved quickly, entering the other room as the adults watched, transfixed. I tried to twist in Jimmy's hold so I could reassure Tanner and Emma, tell them to go with the unknown Atlan warlords looking for them, but I heard a sweet voice and sagged in relief.

"Woof! You're here!" Tanner's singsong voice sounded pleased, but Wulf didn't take his eyes off me.

"Go with my friends, Tanner. Take your sister." Wulf's no-nonsense order must have sunk in because Tanner didn't even try to argue.

"Okay. Come on, Emma," Tanner said as if he were one of the full-grown Atlans and not four years old.

"Get my children out of here," Wulf ordered.

My children. He'd called them *my children.*

The two Atlans said something to Tanner and Emma, something I didn't hear, but the children didn't make a sound as the warriors carried them out of sight, to safety. Two more Atlans entered the childcare room and directed the caregivers to take the children somewhere else. Somewhere safe.

Somewhere they wouldn't see what happened next.

Jimmy wasn't waiting for that. He was backing away from Wulf and the other Atlans, gun to my head, dragging me with him. "Stay back. I'm not bluffing. I *will* kill her."

Wulf held up his hands, dropped his weapon and motioned for the other Atlans to step back. "Protect the humans. I will deal with the threat to my mate."

"No, Wulf! Don't," I begged.

What the hell was he doing? He was unarmed! Walking toward a madman with a gun.

"Be still, Olivia." Wulf took a step forward, hands up in front of him as if surrendering. "Release my mate and I will allow the human authorities to deal with you."

"If I don't?" Jimmy asked. "If I blow her fucking head off?"

"If you harm her, I will pull your head from your spine and watch your blood soak the ground." Wulf's voice was deep, feral. I had never heard that tone before. He meant every word. But he was still... Wulf. His beast was there beneath the surface. I could see the struggle in Wulf's eyes, but he was holding on. For me.

"Just let me go, Jimmy," I told him. "It's not worth it."

"Why do you have a gun? Do what he says, James." Jimmy's father's voice was stern, but he sounded confused. Could the old man really be that ignorant of what his wife and son were doing in the world?

Jimmy stepped back. I stumbled against him, and he yanked me. Hard. The gun dug into my temple, and tears filled my eyes. I was trying not to panic, but seeing Wulf take another step, hands still in the air, made me want to scream.

"You really are a stupid animal, aren't you?" Jimmy moved the gun from my temple to point at Wulf... and fired.

"No!" I screamed, struggling in his hold until I glanced at my hand and realized I still held the crystal goblet. With every ounce of strength I possessed, I flung my arm back and smashed the crystal on top of Jimmy's head just as the gun went off again.

"You bitch." Jimmy cursed but his hold broke and I pulled away, stumbling as far from him as I could get.

Wulf moved so fast I registered his roar before I figured out he already had Jimmy in his hands. My tormentor stared at me with round eyes, his gaze full of pain and horror as Wulf placed one hand on his shoulder, one under his jaw and...pulled.

Agnes screamed. Harold shouted. The Atlans in the room watched stoically, making no sound, as Wulf ripped Jimmy's head back and up. The sound of tearing flesh made me gag, and I looked away when the crackling of Jimmy's spine breaking and popping free filled the room.

Everyone in the room screamed and gasped in horror.

I didn't need to see the headless corpse to believe Jimmy was dead. I didn't want to see it.

"You bastard! I'll have your head for this!" Senator Jenaway raged, her voice a high-pitched wail. The sound made my spine stiffen, and I turned to face her.

"No, Agnes, I will have your head," I said to the woman, suddenly calm. "I know every drug dealer Jimmy uses. Every drop. I know you were behind everything. I'm sure the police will be very interested in what I have to say. You are finished."

Harold paled, leading his wife away, as if fleeing now would wash away what she'd done. Both of them looked older and much more fragile than they had mere moments ago. Seeing your son's head ripped off might do that.

Walter and Marcia were nowhere to be seen, and I didn't much care what happened to them.

Wulf, my Wulf, stood before me, bleeding. I blinked, remembered Jimmy had shot him. Twice.

I ran to him and wanted to jump into his arms but

stopped directly before him. "Oh my God, Wulf. You're hurt."

He shook his head. "No. I am not human or Atlan, mate. Not anymore." He gently cupped my face, and I stared up at him, at the side of his face that had been scored by Jimmy's first shot.

"He shot you. In the face."

"Watch." Wulf stood silently, and I did as he asked. I stared as his skin knit itself back together, as the bullet wound in his shoulder stopped bleeding, then ejected the bullet. Within moments he looked uninjured. Healed. I took a clean napkin from the table, dabbed it in water and wiped the blood from his cheek. Nothing. There was no sign of any kind of wound. His skin was perfect.

"I... I don't understand."

"The integrations, mate. I am not what I once was." He leaned down and rested his forehead on mine. "Why did you leave?"

I knew he spoke of the program. "I thought you wanted her."

He shook his head. "Never. I am yours, Olivia."

"What about Ruth... and the cuffs?"

"The show was holding my cuffs hostage. I wanted to fling Ruth off my lap, and I did, but I wanted the cuffs in my hands first. I was done with their antics. It was clear the producer had planned it all to pull out my beast. For the... ratings."

I nodded, understanding.

"As soon as Chet gave me the cuffs, I stood, untangled myself from Ruth Sanchez and went after you."

He patted his side, and I looked down, saw that his cuffs were there, clipped to his waist.

For the first time I really, truly believed him. "Okay."

Dead body on the floor, blood on my hand, blood on Wulf's clothing. I didn't care. He was mine, and I was going to keep him. "I'll take the mating cuffs now."

He led me a short distance away—ignoring the chaos of the room around us—and knelt, held out the cuffs and his wrists. Head bent, he waited.

One of the nearest Atlans cleared his throat. "If you deem him worthy, you must claim him by placing the mating cuffs on his wrists."

I shook with nerves, maybe crazy adrenaline, but I managed to reach for the large cuffs and wrap first one, then the second around his wrists. When he looked up at me with pure lust, adoration, devotion—he hid nothing from me—I nearly lost it. "I think I love you, Wulf," I admitted. Finally.

"I love you, Olivia Mercier," he replied, his voice a deep, beasty growl. "I choose you. My beast chooses you." He took the smaller cuffs and demanded I hold out my wrists. "You are mine now and forever."

"Okay." I was well past arguing against something I wanted so desperately. Happiness I'd never imagined coursed through me.

"Let's go home." He stood, kissed me gently and placed a small round device on my gown.

I looked down at it. Frowned. "What's this?"

"A transport beacon," he replied. "This will enable us to transport directly to The Colony. It is how Warden Egara transported the Atlan guards from the processing center to me in such a short time. She sent ones for Tanner and Emma as well."

"What about Lucy?" I asked. "She can't stay here. Not with Jimmy's mom still on the loose."

He lifted his head and nodded to the nearest Atlan. "The

female, Lucy Vandermark, is wounded and recovering at the hotel. Please make sure she is safely transported to The Colony and will arrive when we do."

"Yes, Commander."

"I am not a commander," Wulf corrected. "Not anymore."

"Yes, Commander." The younger Atlan grinned and took off before Wulf could correct him again.

"So, Lucy can come too?" I asked, worried for my BFF. I couldn't leave her here on Earth.

He nodded solemnly. "Yes. She is part of your family and will be protected. You will all receive your NPUs when we arrive."

I sagged against him, wrapping my arms around his waist because I could. "Thank you."

He lifted me in his arms—which felt incredible—and carried me out of the building. People made a path for us; no one dared stop the warlord. "You never need thank me for taking care of what's mine."

I nuzzled his neck and decided that sounded pretty damn good to me. He tapped something on his wrist, and a female voice filled the air.

"How did it go, Wulf?"

"Very well, Warden Egara," Wulf said, not stopping until we stood in front of the two Atlans who held the children.

The warlords' usually severe expressions held wide smiles as Emma patted her warlord's head.

"I thank you for your assistance."

"Of course," she replied. "Is your bride with you? And the children? Does she have the mating cuffs on? Are you all ready to go?"

Wulf smiled down at me, then set me on my feet. He went to the Atlans, took Emma from one and handed her to me. I snuggled her close and kissed her sweet head. Then he took Tanner from the other and offered his thanks to the duo. "All your requirements have been met, Warden. We are ready to transport."

"Excellent. Olivia?"

I raised my head in surprise at the voice coming from Wulf's wrist called my name. "Yes?"

"Your new life on The Colony will begin in 3...2...1..."

I held on to my beast as everything went black.

16

I BLINKED, then again. The familiar gray walls of the transport room on Base 3 surrounded us. The air felt different. Drier. Cooler. The scent was familiar. Fuck, I was back. Less than thirty days after I left, *everything* had changed. I was supposed to find a mate, but I'd found an entire family. The mating fever was still upon me, but it had driven me to get us here, away from the danger, the insanity, that had followed us on Earth.

I looked down at Tanner, who was unconscious in my arms. It was to be expected with the distance from Earth being so great. I felt the pull of weariness, and I was probably six or seven times his weight. I was used to the sap of energy as I'd transported hundreds of times.

My gaze flicked to Olivia beside me. She was looking at me, eyes wide, and reached out and set her free hand on my arm. I was surprised she was conscious as I'd heard many females from Earth arrived sprawled on the pad. As for Emma in her arms, unconscious as well.

As I'd commanded, the Atlan had found Lucy and given her a transport beacon. Her arrival had been timed to coincide with ours, because she stood beside us.

Lucy took a step, spun in a circle. "Wow."

Thank fuck. We were all here, together. No transport issues, no last bouts of disaster to mar the way. It was over. The mission to Earth complete. I'd come back whole. More than whole.

"Are you both all right?" I asked, wanting to ensure they were well before anything else. I didn't want them fainting and hitting their heads.

"Heck, yeah," Lucy said, grinning. "Just like *Star Trek*. 'Beam me up, Scottie.'"

Down off the transport pad stood Governor Maxim, who held little Max in his arms, Lady Rone, Kiel and Surnan.

I looked to our governor and nodded in respect, but the doctor was the one I needed first. I carried Tanner down the steps and directly over to him. "You have the NPUs ready? It's best to do the insertion now so they're not afraid."

The focused and often rigid doctor nodded. He'd received the request from Warden Egara, for which I was grateful. The small NPU insertion tool, the name of which was lost on me, was already in his hand.

Before I allowed the doctor to begin, I looked to Olivia, who came down the steps to stand beside me. "He wishes to put the NPUs in now while they are still out. Can he do yours first so you can understand?"

She did not know the doctor's language.

"Oh, yes," she allowed.

"Just turn to the side and tilt your head so he can put it by your temple." She did as I said and angled her head. She winced when the implant was inserted, but only for a moment. Surnan turned to Lucy. "And you, please."

"Oh, I understand!" Olivia said, eyes wide.

Lucy frowned.

"It's your turn for your NPU," Olivia offered.

"Oh, great." Lucy bounced over and got into position for Surnan. He was done with her implant in seconds, and she walked off once again to explore.

"It's time for the children's implants," I said.

My cuffs might be on her wrists, but I would look to her for agreement about the children. She nodded and I shifted Tanner so Surnen had access to the side of his head.

WIth a beep of sound, the small chip had been inserted. He waved a wand over him, assessing his health.

"This is my mate, Olivia," I said to everyone in the room as he did so, although I was sure they'd figured it out on their own.

She stepped forward as Surnan looked to her and offered a slight bow. "My lady. The boy is fine. He will awaken soon, eager to see his new home."

Olivia smiled and glanced around at everyone. "Hello. It's nice to have a welcoming committee. This NPU is great."

Lady Rone came over, smiled and stroked Emma's curls. "Wulf went to Earth for a reality show but ended up on a soap opera. Hi, I'm Rachel. I'm so glad you're here."

"That's Tanner and this"—Olivia moved a slumped Emma off her shoulder—"is Emma."

"They won't feel anything," Surnan promised, then inserted the chip behind Emma's little ear. He did a quick health scan of her as well. "She is also healthy, but the transport took all her energy. There is no reason to worry." He put the tool down and took a ReGen wand from his pocket, first waving it over Emma's injection site, then Tanner's. It took all of thirty seconds.

"Finished. They won't even know of the implants."

"Thank you, Doctor," I said.

"May I scan you as well, my lady?" Surnan asked.

I narrowed my eyes, very familiar with Surnan's need to examine all new mates. "She's not a bride," I reminded.

"Surnan has learned his lesson with Mikki," Rachel said with a raised eyebrow.

He held up his hands, the small scanner between his fingers. "A scan only. For your mate and her friend."

I'd forgotten Lucy, who was standing by the transport tech looking at the controls. "This is Lucy Vandermark."

Lucy came over and shook the doctor's hand. "Nice to meet you. You don't look like an Atlan."

He offered her a small smile. "No. I am from Prillon Prime. With your permission, I will scan your health with this wand, ensuring the transport caused no harm."

Lucy studied Surnan. With his gold skin tone and more severe features, he had to be intriguing to her. Plus, his integrations were visible.

"Except for the coloring, you remind me of Spock," she said with a ready smile and a shrug. "Go for it."

He scanned her, then Olivia. Since she stood directly beside me, his scan picked up some of my data as well. "Warlord, you still have a fever." His gaze dropped to my cuffs, his relief visible when he confirmed they were on my wrists.

"Yes, my mating fever is still upon me. I have yet to claim my mate."

He took a step back, as if my beast was going to come out and rip his head off. "You must do something about that."

Olivia blushed and I only raised my eyebrow.

"We saw the last show. Oh my God, I have to ensure that Ruth Sanchez woman doesn't get a second chance at finding a match," Rachel said, worry lacing her voice.

I thought of Ruth, of her vindictive, manipulative ways. I had no idea why I'd been so upset she'd rejected me. Looking back, I considered myself fortunate.

Maxim joined his wife, and little Max patted her shoulder. Rachel lifted his hand and kissed the palm. "I saw her antics. We can't judge her for her behavior. The second test, if she chose to volunteer, would put her once again with an Atlan who could tame her wild ways."

"More likely she'd end up on Trion over her mate's knee," Kiel said, coming to join us.

I couldn't argue with him. I was thankful Ruth Sanchez wasn't mine.

"What about the show?" Olivia asked.

Rachel huffed out a laugh. "After Wulf stormed off—again—Chet Bosworth spoke about how he really must have met his mate in you, Olivia. He got all gushy and sappy, and the audience ate it up. I did. I spoke with Warden Egara. The plan is to interview her about how all transported here, together. A happy ending."

She sighed.

I frowned. "What of the mess at the ball?" I asked, worried it might adversely affect females from volunteering —my ultimate reason for going to Earth in the first place.

Maxim took a step toward us. "It's still being cleaned up."

Right, we'd transported directly from the event.

"You'll be a hero, ridding Earth of a drug kingpin who'd wreaked havoc on the entire eastern seaboard of the United States, or so I've been told."

"I am not a hero. I wanted my mate."

Rachel grinned and pointed at me. "That's why women are going to line up to get tested. Nice job, hot stuff."

Tanner began to stir in my arms, then lifted his head. "Woof, are we at your house now?"

He looked around the room, his eyes wide. "Hi! I'm Tanner from Erf."

Surnan smiled at him. "There are other boys and girls here who are eager to meet you."

Tanner popped right up in my hold as if he'd been reinflated with energy. "There are?"

"I have a boy who is a little older than you," Kiel said. "His name is Wyatt. I've told him about you, and he should be here—"

The transport room door slid open and in raced Wyatt. His mother, Lindsey, was a few seconds behind. The boy was human, and if I remembered correctly, around six or seven years old.

"—right now."

"My dad said a boy was coming from Earth!" Wyatt said, wiggling around and practically bursting with excitement. He was missing his top two front teeth.

Tanner wiggled in my hold, and I lowered him to his feet. "I'm Tanner and I'm four." He patted his chest.

"I'm Wyatt and I was born on Earth. Then I came here to live, like you. I'm digging for dinosaur bones. Want to help?"

Tanner spun around and looked up at Olivia. "You have dinosaurs here?"

"Not real ones. I like to pretend."

"Can I? Can I?" Tanner asked.

At the sound of his loud, eager voice, Emma woke up, glanced around and blinked.

Tanner's face, that happiness, filled me with joy. It wouldn't ease the fever like Olivia could, but it definitely settled my restless spirit. His wonder and excitement at the world around him—whether it was on Earth or on The Colony—was infectious. It wasn't something I wanted Surnen to cure.

"I'm Lindsey." She came over and set a hand on Wyatt's shoulder. "It's fine if Tanner goes with us. By the look of it, it would go bad if he didn't. I'm sure you've got things to do."

Lindsey grinned and it seemed like everyone knew my business.

"Oh, um. Sure," Olivia replied.

"Tanner," I said.

He looked up at me. "Do you remember playing Hunter the other day?"

He nodded, his hair flopping over his forehead.

"Wyatt's father is that guy." I pointed at Kiel. "He's Everian, as I told you about, and the best Hunter I know. I bet he and Wyatt can teach you some things."

His mouth fell open, and he stared at Kiel wide-eyed. Kiel, who was a quiet male by nature, grinned down at Tanner and fluffed his hair. "Come on, Earthling. Wulf's going to show your mother your new quarters. Maybe you can spend the night with Wyatt, and he can show you around. All right?"

Tanner could only nod, then looked up at Olivia. She was still his touchstone. She bent down and kissed his head. "Digging for dinosaur bones and learning how to hunt?"

He nodded, wiggled some more.

"Have fun," she murmured. "Good manners!"

He and Wyatt tore out of the transport room at warp speed. Everyone laughed at their enthusiasm and easy bond. Kiel took Lindsey's hand, and they walked toward the exit. "We'll watch him," he said, looking over his shoulder. "Don't worry. Get rid of that fever."

"Yes, Warlord," Maxim added, patting his son on the back. "As your governor, I order you to take your mate to your quarters and claim her. End that mating fever. Finally."

I couldn't help but grin, and my beast circled and practically snarled at me to take her already.

"We'll take Emma," Rachel said, eyes full of hope because I had a feeling she had a desire for another child, and a girl at that. "Max is a little younger, but we've got toys and things to keep her entertained. Also, our quarters are very toddler-proof."

"She's a little clingy. I don't want her to fuss the whole time," Olivia advised, stroking Emma's hair. While Tanner hadn't been shy, Emma was.

"I'm a familiar face," Lucy said, coming over to Olivia and holding out her hands. Emma leaned toward her and went willingly into Lucy's arms. "See? We'll have fun on a new planet, won't we? Maybe we can find a growly beast for me?" Lucy asked Emma, who giggled.

Lucy turned and started toward the exit, although she had no idea where she was going. I had to remember to thank her later. Claiming a mate in beast mode wasn't easy to accomplish with small children.

"All settled then. Have fun!" Rachel said, waggling her eyebrows. She made it halfway to the door, then turned around. "Oh, Wulf. Thank you for doing such a good job on Earth. It didn't go as expected... but I think it turned out pretty darn well."

Maxim slung his free arm over her shoulder, and they waited for my response.

I glanced down at Olivia. "Yes. It turned out pretty darn well."

"Claim the woman," Maxim said again.

I didn't have to be told twice. Jimmy Steel was dead.

Ruth Sanchez was light-years away. The *Bachelor Beast*, Chet Bosworth and all the insanity from the past few weeks were left behind on Earth. I had my mate, I had the children—who were being well observed—and it was time.

I turned to fully face Olivia, bending at the waist so we were eye level. I cupped her face in my hands. "Are you all right with the children going off with the others? I know you don't know them, but I trust them with my life. Lindsey is the one who organized the *Bachelor Beast* and my being the one sent to Earth. I should yell at her, but honestly I'm thankful. I have you. Tanner and Emma. I vow that they will be fine while I claim you."

Her eyes searched mine and she nodded. "I know. I want you to claim me. Please? I don't want to wait."

My beast agreed and growled at the way she begged. My mind flashed to earlier when she stood before Jimmy Steel, his dirty hands on her. My beast was fierce but weak for her. We had to know she was whole. Safe. Ours. To do that, I would feel her heat surround my cock, feel her lush curves beneath the press of my body. I'd fill her with my cum and my beast would growl and finally... finally be at peace.

Leaning down, I tossed Olivia over my shoulder and carried her out of the room, my hand on her ass.

"Wulf!" she cried, laughing.

"You're mine, Olivia, and it's time to prove it."

———

OLIVIA

I HAD no idea how long he carried me, but all I could feel was how strong he was. My hands were on his lower back and butt, and I felt the play of muscles with every step. I caught the glint of the cuffs and smiled. I couldn't see anything of my new home, only a hallway floor that went on and on. I saw other people's legs, so I knew there were others around, but Wulf made no effort to speak to anyone or make introductions.

A door slid open, and Wulf stepped inside, then carefully lowered me to my feet. With a big hand on my waist, he ensured I wasn't light-headed before he kissed me. Right there. I had to assume we were in his quarters, but I couldn't see anything around him.

Not that I cared. The kiss was like a match, and it lit a flame inside me. No, not a flame, an inferno. There had been the show and Ruth's... well, bitchiness. Then Jimmy Steel. Wulf had been shot. Shot! I'd been on an emotional roller coaster, but now we were here on The Colony. Safe and together.

Tanner and Emma were having fun and, well, not here. I could have sex with Wulf and not have to keep quiet. There was no way on Earth... ha! There was no way I could do that. Not this time. Not when I knew this was for real. That he was mine.

His hands cupped my cheeks, and I reached up, held his wrists. Felt the cuffs around them.

"Wulf," I whispered against his lips. "I need you."

A growl rumbled from his chest, and beneath my palms I felt him grow. Pulling back, I watched, as I had on the show, as he turned into his beast. His clothes tore, his muscles and bones somehow magically grew bigger, longer. Harder. It amazed me how tall he became. I had to tilt my head so far back to meet his wild, feral eyes.

"Mine," he breathed. His chest heaved, and he watched me. Waited.

"Yes. Yes, Wulf, I'm yours."

There was nothing else to say. I belonged to him in all ways. He'd proven himself to belong to me. Now I would give myself to him in his claiming. He needed it to survive. Just as he'd risked his life for me back in New York, I would give mine to him. To heal. To be whole.

He grabbed me by the hips and picked me up, walked until I was pressed against the wall. It was like the back room the other night. Pinned. Lucy had said Atlans claimed their females standing. Well, his beast was claiming me now.

God, yes.

I was hot all over, the need for him making me frantic, and I didn't have an inner beast. I understood his need to feel closer, to connect with me in the most elemental way.

My clothing, the beautiful dress I never wanted to see again, was torn away, falling to the floor, but I didn't pay any attention. His hands were on me. His mouth. I felt the press of his body, the thrust of his hips at my center. I rocked into him, needing more contact.

Hoisting me higher, he took my nipple into his mouth, sucked and tugged, nipped with his teeth. His other hand cupped and played with my other breast, and I was pinned in place with his hips.

"More, Wulf. More." I tugged at his hair, pulling him closer.

Our breathing was all that could be heard. I felt him work down his pants, and the hot prod of his cock was at my entrance.

He lifted his head, looked me in the eye. I saw the need, the heat, the raging passion that was focused all on me.

"Mine." His hands slid up my arms, pushed them over my head so my wrists were pinned in his grip.

With that one word, he pulled me down onto him as he thrust deep.

I arched my back, cried out at the feel of him. So big. So deep. I was wet for him, dripping, and had eased his way, but his cock was impressive.

He didn't hold back now. I knew he couldn't. I didn't want him to. I wanted everything from him. All Wulf.

"Yes!" I cried, my head falling back against the wall as he took me. I could do nothing but feel. The strength of him. The thrust of his cock as he mastered my body. The sound of him, fierce snarls and groans. The heat from his skin made me sweat.

But it was the connection I'd never felt before. Never imagined could be between two people.

"I'm going to come. Oh God!" I rippled around him and then came, white lights dancing before my eyes as I screamed his name, over and over like a mantra.

I felt him thicken within me, throb, and as he thrust deep one last time, he roared. I would swear the walls shook, that the entire base knew Wulf had come, filling me with his seed. Ending his fever, soothing his beast and making me his. Finally.

His warm breath fanned my neck as he held me in place. He was still hard inside me, filling me, but I could feel the cum seep from me. Claiming was a messy, sweaty business, but it made me smile.

"When I can feel my fingers, let's do that again," I said.

He lifted his head, looked at me. He wasn't recovered. In fact, he looked overcome. As if he'd spurted his life force into my pussy. Slowly he lowered my arms and kissed me. Gently. Sometime during my recovery, his beast had diminished and he was Wulf again. All sweaty brow and stunned look.

"Again. And again. We have all night."

I stroked his damp hair as I met his dark gaze. Shook my head. "We have the rest of our lives. Mate."

He turned and carried me through his quarters to a bed, laid me upon it. "The rest of our lives," he repeated, his cock still deep. He pulled back, then thrust again, making me cry out in pleasure. "But we'll start now."

A SPECIAL THANK YOU TO MY READERS...

Want more? I've got **hidden** bonus content on my web
site *exclusively* for those on my mailing list.

If you are already on my email list, you don't need to do a thing!
Simply scroll to the bottom of my newsletter emails and click on
the *super-secret* link.

Not a member? What are you waiting for? In addition to ALL of
my bonus content (great new stuff will be added regularly) you
will be the first to hear about my newest release the second it hits
the stores—AND you will get a free book as a special welcome gift.

Sign up now! http://freescifiromance.com

FIND YOUR INTERSTELLAR MATCH!

YOUR mate is out there. Take the test today and discover your perfect match. Are you ready for a sexy alien mate (or two)?

VOLUNTEER NOW!

interstellarbridesprogram.com

.

DO YOU LOVE AUDIOBOOKS?

Grace Goodwin's books are now available as audiobooks...everywhere.

LET'S TALK SPOILER ROOM!

Interested in joining my **Sci-Fi Squad**? Meet new like-minded sci-fi romance fanatics and chat with Grace! Get excerpts, cover reveals and sneak peeks before anyone else. Be part of a private Facebook group that shares pictures and fun news! Join here:

https://www.facebook.com/groups/scifisquad/

***

Want to talk about Grace Goodwin books with others? Join the **SPOILER ROOM** and spoil away! Your GG BFFs are waiting! (And so is Grace)

Join here:

https://www.facebook.com/groups/ggspoilerroom/

GET A FREE BOOK!

JOIN MY MAILING LIST TO BE THE FIRST TO KNOW OF NEW RELEASES, FREE BOOKS, SPECIAL PRICES AND OTHER AUTHOR GIVEAWAYS.

http://freescifiromance.com

ALSO BY GRACE GOODWIN

Cyborg Seduction

Her Cyborg Beast

Cyborg Fever

Rogue Cyborg

Cyborg's Secret Baby

Her Cyborg Warriors

The Colony Boxed Set 1

Interstellar Brides® Program: The Virgins

The Alien's Mate

His Virgin Mate

Claiming His Virgin

His Virgin Bride

His Virgin Princess

Interstellar Brides® Program: Ascension Saga

Ascension Saga, book 1

Ascension Saga, book 2

Ascension Saga, book 3

Trinity: Ascension Saga - Volume 1

Ascension Saga, book 4

Ascension Saga, book 5

Ascension Saga, book 6

Faith: Ascension Saga - Volume 2

Ascension Saga, book 7

Ascension Saga, book 8

Ascension Saga, book 9

Destiny: Ascension Saga - Volume 3

ABOUT GRACE

Grace Goodwin is a USA Today and international bestselling author of Sci-Fi and Paranormal romance with more than one million books sold. Grace's titles are available worldwide in multiple languages in ebook, print and audio formats. Two best friends, one left-brained, the other right-brained, make up the award-winning writing duo that is Grace Goodwin.

They are both mothers, escape room enthusiasts, avid readers and intrepid defenders of their preferred beverages. (There may or may not be an ongoing tea vs. coffee war occurring during their daily communications.) Grace loves to hear from readers!

All of Grace's books can be read as sexy, stand-alone adventures. But be careful, she likes her heroes hot and her love scenes hotter. You have been warned...

www.gracegoodwin.com
gracegoodwinauthor@gmail.com